The

BEAUTY

of the

WORLD

"*The Beauty of the World* has a decidedly film-like quality to it, with a terse, present-tense narrative, brisk pace and diagram-like detail that suggest a scenario. It also has the attractive young characters that the movies thrive on."

Martin Morrow – FAST FORWARD WEEKLY

"The beauty exists in Newman's juxtaposition of fear and peace: a journalist noticing the harsh beauty of a desert landscape while being pursued by enemy soldiers or a man remarking on the childlike visage of his sleeping lover while both are being held in an internment camp. More than a political indictment or a grieving testimony, The Beauty of the World, allows the complexities of humanity to come through on every page. Newman does not shy away from showing the joy that pervades even the most abject of human misery allowing both her characters and her novel to embrace all that exists in the world."

Amber Cowie - THE VERMILION STANDARD

"Newman's telling of this story clearly echoes the kind of writing that would, if it were not fiction, be a major human-interest story in some national news magazine. It is immediate and urgent, complex and yet matter-of-fact. The characters come across as real, flawed, no stand-ins for abstract ideas."

Steven Laird - Editor for *Lichen Arts & Letters Preview*

'*The Beauty of the World* is a captivating tale of courage and determination that takes a look at the tragedy of war....Newman skilfully juggles several overlapping narratives and goes back and forth in time to tell us the story of Emil and his fiancé, then returning to the present....Newman's style is honest and direct. The novel jumps into the action from the very first page and stays an enjoyable read right through the end, constantly keeping us on the edge of our seat."

Laila Maalouf – for VIA Destinations Magazine

July 2022

The Beauty of the World

by Stacey Newman

To my beautiful, brilliant niece, love you so much,

Auntie

Stacey

xo

WINGATE PRESS
Stratford, Canada

Library and Archives Canada Cataloguing in Publication:

Newman, Stacey Lynn, 1974-
    The beauty of the world / written by Stacey Lynn Newman.

ISBN 0-9738565-3-X

    I. Title.

PS8627.E93B42 2006   C813'.6   C2006-901140-0

Layout design by Wingate Press
Cover Design by Wingate Press
Edited by Allyson Latta
Cover artwork by Lara Chauvin www.larachauvin.com

Published by:

Wingate Press
www.wingatepress.com

We acknowledge the support of the Canada Council for the Arts which last year invested $20.0 million in writing and publishing throughout Canada.

**Canada Council
for the Arts**

**Conseil des Arts
du Canada**

Printed in Canada

To Stephen

"It is easier to square the circle than to get round a mathematician."

- Augustus de Morgan

The BEAUTY *of the* WORLD

"The beauty of the world which is so soon to perish, has two edges, one of laughter, one of anguish, cutting the heart asunder."

Virginia Woolf

Prologue

There is a war in this place.

Where the mountains slip into foothills, on the periphery of alpine evergreen and deciduous forests, the desert begins. Titian sand rises into bluffs that sharply plunge into nothingness. This desert has carefully embraced the Republic of Perda—its mountains and its people, for centuries. The desert air is cool and dry. It will barely snow anywhere but high in the mountains, where the peaks are normally tipped with white. Elsewhere in this landlocked nation, precipitation is unpredictable. It can come in the form of quiet drizzle, or in torrential downpours that swamp the plains and cause flash floods in the desert.

In the Republic of Perda, Bellona Adalardo is leading her country on a self-destructive course. Arrogance has blinded this goddess of war. She cannot know that the coming occupation—an occupation that she has agreed to and helped to design—of her nation will not be carried out as such. It will be an invasion, during which tens of thousands Perdans will be killed. She has given up many secrets to the foreign occupiers. The Adalardo government has publicly promoted this occupation for the purpose of economic stability while privately ensuring great personal gain by the government's largest financiers, for this has become a corrupt and damaged institution deluded by greed and by its pursuit of power, like so many governments before it. It has made the fatal mistakes of betraying its people—who are vociferously opposed to the occupation and ignored by the regime they elected—and of overestimating its position in this growing conflict.

Rolling hills spread across the horizon. Their darkest orange profiles are darkened in the low, western light. Their yawning shadows are interspersed with the machinery and the commotion of conflict. Dark greens and light browns move across the earth—scurrying, burying, loathing and conditioned for war. Fear, once based in a precarious economic climate, is now motivated by half-truths-turned-military-intelligence.

The soldiers are prepared. This region, once foreign to them, has become intimately entwined with their destinies, and the destinies of the people of Perda, from whom they have been told to expect resistance and extreme violence.

Perda is suspended from the beauty of the world.

§

Sophie is a journalist. She is courageous. But even the bravest have moments of weakness and fear, moments in which they want desperately to revert to the beliefs of their childhoods. Even the strongest, most unmovable beings were children once. Their mothers and fathers held them and made them believe that with words and reason all fears might be dispelled.

Sophie has been covering politics in the Republic of Perda for many weeks, in the capital city of Buena Gente. The city offers beautiful vistas. Mountains—the Colinas del Fuegos—separate the densely populated areas of the Republic from the stark, desert regions to the far north in the country. The well-populated city is surrounded by dense forest that gives way to fertile agricultural land in the foothills of the Colinas del Fuegos.

Perda's climate is cold temperate, and Buena Gente boasts pleasant weather during most of the year, with cool nights and warm or hot days in the spring and summer, and cold, clear autumns and winters. Tourists visit the country to take historic tours of renowned clay edifices and villages built centuries before. Buena Gente's modern attractions include an annual cosmopolitan fashion festival, art galleries, cafés and the other hallmarks of a bustling urban centre.

But now, many of the buildings have been destroyed. Also gone are the ruins of ancient civilizations—obliterated in the attacks on the northern region.

Sophie is crawling, the bullets rushing overhead as she scrapes her belly and the fronts of her thighs against the gravel- and debris-covered street of the downtown area. She shouts to her colleague. Tom Ransley is following closely behind her. The sound of gunfire echoes deceitfully so that it is impossible to know from which direction it is coming. Pulling her arms underneath her chest and raising herself on her elbows, she looks back and sees Tom on the ground, partially beneath the truck that was supposed to have sheltered them. He has been struck by one of the bullets that was not intended for him but which found him nonetheless. His face looks upwards strangely. Blood has collected in the corner of his mouth and farther down his slack jaw. His chest does not rise or fall. His eyes are open, fixed and devastated.

Sophie feels smothered. What air her lungs still hold, they refuse to release. She is unaware of anything but Tom's body and her sudden solitude.

She is afraid.

She has not been afraid before on assignment, but this is her first war experience as a reporter. She knows she is only in Perda because her colleagues refused to come. There is a growing boycott by journalists around the world against coverage of this invasion in any capacity other than freelance.

Sophie agrees with the boycott. Historically it is unprecedented. Their refusal to cover this event under the direction of biased networks is meant to stall the propaganda machine that many of them have inadvertently contributed to building.

This has become a personal journey. The pull to Perda was strong. She jumped at the chance to come here, to the place where her grandparents were born—an opportunity that meant everything to her. Her grandparents were proud of her. They were always proud of her, no matter what. Their involvement in her life was pivotal after the death of her parents when she was just seventeen. And now her grandparents are also gone. First her grandma, quietly, peacefully. And Sophie was not surprised that her grandfather followed soon after. Sophie knows about loss, she understands it, her identity has been formed out of loss, her unwillingness to become close to anyone, or anything, was formed out of the profound fear that she has developed— the fear of losing those closest to her. In this place, Tom was closest to her, her friend, her colleague for three years. And he is gone now too.

Sophie can't reconcile *this* Perda with her imagined Perda, the Perda she heard stories of during her childhood. In her mind, in her grandfather's stories, this country was a sanctuary filled with lush natural beauty and centuries of history preserved in ancient ruins. Sophie saw the beauty of Perda poured out beneath her as the airplane descended. It was as though it was welcoming her home. But once she was on the ground, her ideas of Perda began to change. This country has been ravaged in a few short weeks of conflict. Sophie is thankful that her grandparents are not alive to see this.

Dread pervades her thoughts. She is inexperienced, trapped, and alone in the middle of a war zone that was not so long ago relatively undisturbed. She sits next to the warm body of her friend and colleague as she stares at the remains of shops, restaurants and bakeries that line the streets. Their windows still advertise fresh delicacies and select local coffees. Coffee is one of Perda's main exports, along with Perda's coveted natural resources.

Behind the windows that are not broken are the burnt remains of everything and everyone caught inside the buildings when the bombs were dropped. The walls next to the windows are covered with posters. The name of the occupying forces hovers over empty words promising wealth and freedom. The scene is surreal, incomprehensible—the remnants of ordinary belie the surrounding chaos.

Sophie now understands that this is not a country begging for freedom. Perda has experienced many internal struggles, for it is a small country that is of great interest to outside influences. These interests have found their way into the hearts of Perdans, many of whom have developed opposing ideas with regard to the management of Perda's resources. Violence had erupted many times during the last fifty years, amongst various factions.

Perda's problems are increasing, its people angry, but its spirit is far from crushed and far from requiring deliverance. Sophie now believes, as many do, that the war has been externally instigated—the fire was set intentionally. It now burns of its own volition, creates its own weather and destroys everything it encounters. The arsonists are proud of their accomplishment. They are unaware of the force they have ignited.

The tears come. Sophie sits against the vehicle, facing Tom's body. An explosion sounds, at least a block away but the blast shakes the buildings around her and throws dust into the air. Sophie falls backward; her head hits the side of the vehicle. She leans forward for a moment. She is dizzy, but despite her confusion, she reaches into Tom's vest for the cellular phone. It isn't there. She searches his other pockets. Nothing. She presses her palm against his eyes until they are closed. She holds his hand and can't seem to let go. His skin is still warm. She knows it could have been her. Tom is gone, though she was speaking to him just moments earlier.

Sophie stays low to the ground. She pulls herself to the lee of a pillar in front of a nearby building. The sound of distant fighting continues to resonate against the buildings.

The air is heavy with the emissions from burning fuel and other unknown materials—particles choke her nose and throat. As a group of soldiers streams past the building, she stays low and still.

She is in a section of the city that is occupied by a violent, insular militia. But there are many groups to account for in this conflict. The Alianza Central de Perda, the ACP—also opposed to the occupation, but organized and large—holds sections of the country outside Buena Gente with unparalleled passion. Then there are the occupying forces, their soldiers highly trained, lethal and suggestible. Finally, there are the reformists, the idealists—their objections in line with those of the ACP, but through political means instead of military brawn—they *were* peaceful, well-funded, and powerful because of their connections, but only as a preventive organization. Once the invasion began, the reformists were displaced, and disconnected from one another, their cause to be carried on by the ACP because the path of least resistance had not been selected by the foreign aggressors. The stories Sophie has already collected speak of horrors, desperation and goodness on all sides of this conflict.

This conflict seems more real to her in this terrible moment than she could have ever imagined. Sophie cannot move. She sits forward, hugging her knees, barely taking in any air for fear that the slightest escaped breath might draw attention to her. But she has been seen, and she feels the man beside her before his hand covers her mouth. He is telling her to be quiet, calm and that he won't hurt her. She struggles against the man as he pulls her to her feet, his hand holding her face, her back, pressed against him, and his other arm pulling her along the wall until they come to a recessed portion of the building's facade.

The man wants to help her, for they are both trapped by the violence that has erupted around their location. But he must keep this journalist quiet. If she draws attention to them, they'll both be killed, without question. "We have to get away from this building." He instructs her as he loosens his grip but keeps his hand against her mouth. He is afraid that she will cry out and that they will be killed, or taken hostage by the soldiers at the checkpoint nearby. He knows this journalist. He has seen her on television. Sophie Panos. He does not want to hurt her, but he understands that she cannot know this.

Sophie is startled, unsure whether he is speaking truthfully. She is pulled around the corner of the building in the direction of a small military truck. The truck is idling, but unoccupied. A group of men with weapons stand across the street from the vehicle, shouting at one another. Dust is still suspended in the air, enough to obscure a clear assessment of their number.

The man sees the truck idling. It is their only chance. They must steal the truck. "Try the back door, I'll watch them."

Cautiously, Sophie steps away from him. She hunches over and approaches the rear passenger door of the vehicle. She opens the door quietly. The man pushes her into the truck. He understands how frightened she must be. He enters the vehicle by the front passenger door. In a swift movement, he is in the driver seat, and they are moving.

"Do up your belt!" he shouts over the sound of gunfire discharged from the group behind them.

Sophie complies, ducking and holding her head against her knees as bullets strike the back and sides of the truck. A shot pierces the rear window, the sound is almost comical, a tiny thud and a whir. The bullet lodges in the dash, resulting in a spray of wire bits and plastic shards throughout the vehicle.

"Are you all right?" Sophie asks. She lifts her head only slightly.

"Yes. Stay down. We are almost out of range."

Sophie keeps low, but she sees that the bullet has not shattered the window. Instead, it has left a small, perfectly round hole in the otherwise unbroken glass. Nausea overcomes her and she vomits in the backseat of the truck.

The man is not concerned with the smell of vomit rising from the back seat. He cannot think of anything but escape. He plans their exit from the city. He will rely on his knowledge of the agricultural region's backroads and their many tributaries.

"We'll be out off this soon." He wants her to understand that he is not going to hurt her.

Sophie looks up at her kidnapper, if that is what he is. He has blood near his right ear. The blood appears to be dry. His hair is dark, but so dishevelled and dirty that she cannot tell if it is truly black. The gunfire continues as they drive farther and farther away from the shooters.

"They won't be close behind—it was a checkpoint, and they only had one vehicle." The man looks at Sophie in the rear view mirror as he speaks.

"Who are you, why have you taken me?" Her throat aches and her voice is hoarse from breathing in the dust.

"I'm not going to hurt you. I was leaving the building when I saw you, but I didn't want to approach, in case you were afraid. You might have called out and drawn attention to us." He pauses and watches her in the rearview mirror. There is no point in giving a false name. She will soon recognize him. That is inevitable. "My name is Emil."

Abruptly, the gunfire stops. By now, they are almost out of the city. The vehicle's tires move erratically over the rough terrain. The road is not much of a road. The pavement soon gives way to dirt and then gravel and stone. The engine is powerful even though the truck is not large, and its heaving, mechanical drone is interrupted periodically by the popping sounds from the tires as they displace stones strewn across the unpaved road. Emil knows a way out of the city, a way they won't be easily followed.

Sophie ascertains concern and perhaps uneasiness, but not violent intent from Emil's eyes as they glance at her sporadically. She cannot see the rest of his face. "I'm Sophie Panos. My colleague was shot just before you grabbed me."

"I know who you are. I've seen you on television, and I heard you on the radio the first night of the strikes. I'm sorry about your colleague." Emil's tone seems sincere.

Sophie turns and looks behind, and feels a surge of panic as the city disappears behind them. "Where are you taking me?"

"I don't know yet," Emil responds truthfully.

"What were you doing in the city?"

"I didn't know where else to go, I needed to think." He sighs.

"About what?"

Emil does not want to talk about Talia. Speaking Talia's name aloud might dissolve the last bit of hope that she is alive. "I was in the apartment building at the corner where you were hiding. I was there for just two days. This morning the explosions started again and they were so close that I decided I had to leave, and that's when I saw you. "

Nothing in her life has prepared Sophie for this. For the loss of her friend in the field. For a situation like this—a contrived conflict in a country that was not previously troubled.

"I want you to bring me back to the city. Please." Sophie hears desperation seeping into her requests.

"You can't go back."

"Why not? I am protected there, and they will be looking for me."

"They'll assume you are dead."

The words seem cruel and indifferent. Her heart is pounding. Her skin is moist and clammy.

Emil pulls the vehicle off the road. They are soon surrounded by forest. The truck grunts and slides as Emil pushes it through dense vegetation. He continues driving until the city is no longer visible. Neither Emil nor Sophie speak for what seems like hours.

§

The sky is tinged red and purple. They are driving away from the setting sun. Sophie has been unresponsive for hours and Emil worries that perhaps she has lost consciousness. He reaches over the seat back and gently shakes her. He is relieved when she moves.

"You have to wake up—we have to get out of the truck." He speaks quietly so as not to frighten her.

Sophie opens her eyes. She is confused, as she does not remember falling asleep. "How far have we come?"

Emil pulls the vehicle to the edge of the thick forest, where the forest dips into a deep, green chasm. "We've been driving for almost four hours. I don't know if they'll come looking for the truck, for us. Maybe. We are stopping here. We have to take some things from the back—water, some weapons."

Sophie sits up and she rubs her face. The acrid odour of vomit emanates from the floor beneath her feet. She isn't feeling as nauseated as she did, but the smell is almost too much. She does her best not to breathe through her nose.

The truck is draped with heavily foliaged vines. Beside the truck, Sophie can see they are near the edge of a canyon or valley of some sort. She pushes herself to the other side of the vehicle and through the window, she peers out onto a ravine, the bottom of which is out of sight. She can see only tree trunks and dense vines near the top of the drop-off. The earth looks hard and dry.

Emil has opened his door. He stares ahead as he speaks.
"Please, get out." The dry soil is disturbed with each breath of
wind that circles the vehicle.

"Why?" Sophie is troubled by Emil's suddenly authoritative
tone.

Emil knows that Sophie will trust him at some point because
she has no choice, and because she will eventually see that he
does not intend to hurt her. He also knows they must get rid of
the truck. It is too easily tracked, and on foot, they can move
into the interior forested areas at the base of the mountains. In
the Colinas del Fuegos—named for their many volcanoes—
there are unguarded borders.

The forest they are in now will soon give way to farmland. They
have to get through the agricultural region in order to reach the
mountains where they will be safer. It will be a very long walk,
difficult in the best of circumstances, but if they stay on the
roads, they will surely be caught.

"We are walking from here. Get out, please." Emil exits the
truck. He walks back and opens her door, then moves around
to the trunk of the vehicle and begins removing contents.

Sophie gets out of the truck unsteadily and watches him as he
pulls a small handgun from the trunk and tucks it into the front
of his jeans. He also pulls out a small dark green box and opens
it. It is filled with plastic water bottles and what looks like a
bottle of something alcoholic—cachaca, a white rum made
from sugar cane. He leaves that bottle in the trunk. Emil places
as many of the plastic water bottles as will fit into a black bag
that he has also taken from the trunk. He places the bag on the
ground.

Sophie cannot clearly see his face. He is moving about purposefully. She follows him away from the truck where he has left the contents he removed. Emil gets back in the truck. Sophie begins to wonder if he is leaving her there after all. Then, unexpectedly, he drives the truck to the side of the ravine, puts something on the floor of the driver's side, and reaches in, and the truck lurches forward, disappears over the edge. The sound of the vehicle falling is less significant than Sophie had expected. There is no immediate explosion. Sophie moves closer to the edge of the ravine. She cannot see into the ravine because of the vegetation, but she hears the sound of metal brushing forcefully against tree branches. There is a loud crash.

Emil turns back toward Sophie. Many hours have passed since they left Buena Gente. In the near twilight, she is able to see how badly his face is bruised and bloodied. His hair is black, his eyes a light hazel colour and his clothes torn and filthy. He is favouring his right arm, holding it as though in pain.

He does not look like a soldier or a combatant at all. There is nothing about him that says he is violent, and although he has expressed numerous concerns, there is nothing vitriolic in his words. His face is kind, and this kindness is unexpected, out of place, confusing. Sophie doesn't know what to do with kindness in a man who recently put his hand over her mouth and dragged her into an unknown wilderness. He is unassuming in blue jeans and a sweater with a blue vest over top, but Sophie suddenly recognizes him. "My God. You are Emil Devante."

Emil looks at Sophie, keeping his expression blank. "Yes. But that doesn't matter now." Emil is obscure intentionally, for he

14

doesn't want Sophie to ask the questions that he dreads most. He is held together by hope and fear and the emotional contest is exhausting. He knows he will soon lose his ability to function if he even considers the possibility that Talia is gone.

"But there must be someone you could have contacted. What about the Adalardo family—surely they could have helped you?" Sophie doesn't understand why Emil didn't use his political ties when he was in trouble. At one point, Bellona Adalardo was the most powerful person in the government. Talia Adalardo—leader of the campaign for reform—although publicly opposed to her mother's government, surely could have aided him in escaping.

Unless Talia has been killed ... Sophie will not ask the question, not yet. She can't find the words. She knows there is a personal connection between Emil and Talia, and she wonders why Talia is not with him.

Sophie's probing deadens Emil further. She can't know that Talia and he are to be married. No one knows of this. But his romantic connection to Talia is otherwise public knowledge. He realizes what Sophie is thinking, she wants to know about Talia, but he won't give her another opportunity to ask about it.

Emil's face hardens, which Sophie accepts as a warning.

"Let's go." He slings the bag over his left shoulder. Then he takes her arm by the elbow and leads her into the trees.

They walk for a long time. Emil's pace is quick and difficult to keep up, but he does not look back to ensure that Sophie is still behind him. The sun has set and the darkness in the forest is deep and watchful. The rising moon provides little light as it filters through the dense canopy. Sophie stays close to Emil for fear of becoming lost as she steps carefully across the hard, coarse ground, lifting her feet over branches and roots. She clumsily grabs onto thin, flexible tree trunks on either side of her for balance as her movements are too fast and too frenzied. The moonlight is reflected off the giant, shiny, seemingly luminous leaves that seem to hang from every tree. The leaves are suspended from vines that drape themselves over any tolerant space in the crowded forest.

Sophie feels childish, useless in this unfamiliar territory. She is confused. *Emil Devante.* Despite who he is, she is frustrated and unnerved by his unwillingness to be honest with her. He has met every one of her questions with determined silence. She doesn't know where she is, nor does she know what to do. Sophie wants to return to the city. She was relatively safe in the city. Her hotel was protected. Though always wary, she had developed a tentative sense of security. And then Tom Ransley was killed, and just like that, everything went to hell.

She needs Emil now, because she doesn't know anything about this region and because he has more of a plan than she is capable of suggesting at this moment. But his identity, his proximity to the Adalardo family, his connections—*if Emil Devante can't get help* ... Sophie realizes that their situation is dire.

Emil has been obviously evasive. This fuels Sophie's anxiety. She wants to trust him: she believes in his politics—the campaign for reform—but he is hiding things from her. Sophie reaches out and she pulls on Emil's upper right arm to stop him from walking.

He flinches and abruptly turns around.

"I'm sorry. Your arm."

He doesn't refer to his injury at all. "We need to keep going." Sophie offers a sarcastic chortle, for he has just confirmed his reluctance to address her concerns. "Why can't we return to the city? Being out here in the middle of nowhere is pointless. And you won't tell me anything … I just don't get it Emil."

Emil doesn't want to upset Sophie, but she should know about the situation. "Your hotel is gone. It was hit this morning, by a mortar round."

Sophie is suspicious. "Why didn't you tell me this before?"

"Would you have believed me?"

"What makes you think I believe you now?"

Emil speaks without any inflection in his voice. "A few of the hotels in the city were hit in an attack. Yours was one of the first, probably because most of the foreign journalists were staying there. The building collapsed. You would have been killed Sophie."

"Why would journalists be targeted?" She asks. "There are so few of us here. You'd think they would want us to get information out, to cover what is truly happening here."

"Obviously someone doesn't like that you're here, or what you've been reporting. Maybe that's why the hotel was hit, to stop the lies. Isn't that the point of the boycott?"

Sophie speaks quietly, despite the anger that she feels toward Emil. "Do you think that I believe in all of this Emil? I'm here because I want to document the occupation and to prove, with *clear* evidence, that it is criminal." Sophie catches her breath. "I thought you were a reformist Emil … peaceful, right? You *understand* their reasons for bombing our hotel?" Sophie takes a step away from Emil. She softens her voice again. "I just want some answers. I'm scared."

Emil is deeply affected by her tone. He should let this go, and so he drops the subject. "I'm sorry Sophie. I'm just ... we need to keep going."

"Wait, how did you know about my hotel?"

"I had a radio. There was a report about the attack on the hotel right after it happened."

She knows he could be lying—but why would he be dishonest? He seems to want to help and she has nothing to offer him. She thinks of the few journalists that she had gotten to know at the hotel and she wonders if they were all killed. It will be assumed that she died there also. No one will be looking for her.

Sophie looks at Emil silently.

"Okay?" he asks her. Although it is more statement than question.

"Yes. Wait, can you give me something to hold on to? I don't want us to be separated in the dark."

"Just stay behind me. I won't lose you." Then he turns away from her and continues on.

Sophie follows as closely as she can.

It has gotten cold. If they were closer to Buena Gente, they would be hearing gunfire and shelling, accompanied by brief flashes of grey-green light and distant thuds. From a distance, the flares of war are almost beautiful. But now Sophie and Emil are too far away from the city to see or hear anything. The air is dry and Sophie is often thirsty, but Emil wants them to conserve water. Once in a while, he takes a sip from a bottle and then passes it back to her before returning the bottle to the bag that he is still carrying. Sophie offers to carry the bag. He slows to pass it to her. She pulls it over her own shoulder; it isn't heavy.

She speaks again as they are walking. "Did they say who was responsible for attacking the hotels?"

"The report was by a local radio station, probably taken over by the occupying forces. They blamed it on the ACP."

"But you don't believe it was the ACP."

"No, but the occupying forces want us to believe it was. Anything to justify the occupation. I think it was the occupying forces that attacked the hotels. There have been so many lies told since the invasion began. But the occupying forces will never admit to going after non-combatants—especially members of the press."

Sophie listens intently, as the sound of Emil's voice is suddenly very distant. "I don't feel well Emil." Sophie is panicked. She feels dizzy again and as though she might faint. She senses a warm rush of liquid from her nose and she tastes blood. Her nose is bleeding profusely. She feels her legs becoming weak beneath her.

"Emil …" She stumbles and falls forward, her arms are wrenched as she hits the dry earth.

Emil crouches next to her. "What's wrong?"

"I'm dizzy. My nose …"

Her lower face is bloody. It is difficult for Emil to see her in the inadequate moonlight, but he can see the dark liquid beneath her nostrils.

"Just let me sit for a minute, please." She squats and leans forward.

"We should find a place to rest. I'll help you walk." He starts to lift her arm.

"You're hurt too ... I can manage." She lifts herself up. She notices that he is holding his arm again.

Sophie tries to stand on her own and walk, but she trips over a fallen branch. Everything spins. Emil pulls her arm over his left shoulder. This time she does not protest. He helps her farther into the dense forest, lowers her against a large tree trunk and, while he holds her head forward and downward, he pinches her nose.

"Were you hurt at all, Sophie? Did you hit your head, or were you struck by anything?"

"There was an explosion. My head was thrown back against the side of a truck."

Emil is worried about her. He can't leave her, but if she is badly injured, she will slow their progress. "You probably have a concussion, but that wouldn't make your nose bleed. The air is very dry and you probably inhaled emissions after the explosion. Keep your head forward." He places his cold hand on the back of her neck.

Sophie feels a bit better. Finally, the bleeding seems to have stopped.

She pushes his hand away. "Emil, you've dragged me out into this forest. I don't have any of my papers. They're probably lost, along with everything else at the hotel. You should have left me where I was, someone would have helped me." She holds her head in her hands. The throbbing continues to nauseate her. She knows that she is being unreasonable, but she is so afraid.

"You would have been killed—the block was surrounded. I don't know how you and your colleague got in there to begin with." Emil is very tired. He looks directly at her and leans in toward her face, which he can hardly see. He wants to get his point across. "Sophie. Why are you really here? How can you watch people dying? Is this your version of making the world a better place?" He doesn't know how a journalist can justify standing, by while people are dying, just for the sake of a good story. He believes that Sophie is well-intentioned, but he has seen the repercussions of allegedly good intentions.

Sophie does not immediately react to his words. She won't break down, because if she does she will die out here. Sophie doesn't want to die. She needs Emil in order to survive.

She believes in her conscience. She knows what is right and what is wrong. She trusts herself and her instincts, and she won't apologize for what she has chosen to do with her life. "This is what I do, Emil. I show people, who think their way of life is the only way of life, that there is another world out there. Where people still fight for survival and where life and death decisions are made daily." Sophie searches for his eyes in the darkness. "Emil, please answer me, what are we doing out here?"

"We are going somewhere safer where we can get information and help." He offers quietly.

She is relieved that he is responding to her.

Emil continues. "The embassies have been empty for weeks now. The city is very unstable. To be safe we have to get out of the country, but the whole region is occupied. The only border areas that are unoccupied are in wilderness areas, in the mountains."

"Why didn't you try to leave Perda earlier?"

"I have family here. I don't know where they are. I hoped they would find me, or that I could get help in Buena Gente."

He is holding something back, so she presses him again and this time she is direct. "Talia? The Adalardos? Where are they now?"

Emil doesn't reply. He looks down, away from her, and then he wipes his face against the palm of his right hand. It is a vulnerable, almost childlike action. Emil's behaviour leaves Sophie feeling bewildered.

She waits a moment before asking again about his injury.

Emil becomes aware that he is rubbing his right shoulder again. But he is weary. "Sophie, please. Just leave it alone for now."

Sophie gives up. Emil is a master at deflection. Right now, it is difficult for her to care about anything except the headache that is slowly consuming her. Her legs ache. She is exhausted in every sense of the word. "I need to close my eyes, Emil. I don't feel well."

"Sleep, then. We should rest for a while anyway." Emil sits beside her, leans back against the tree.

Sophie closes her eyes. She wants escape to come. She wants to forget the events of the day, to forget where she is and the fear and the helplessness that threaten to incapacitate her. She is not courageous, not even close. She is ashamed of herself for feeling this way.

Her immersion in the events of the past weeks has left her feeling that there is the potential for injustice on every side of this war. Only once she had spent time in Perda did she begin to see the truth.

In the past, Sophie has stood over the bodies of other journalists while reporting on such gruesome discoveries. She knows that she may be killed at any moment, and as she closes her eyes, she imagines her own body being discovered in much the same way.

§

Talia holds as many of Emil's fingers as she can reach. The guards are not looking in the direction of the fence. She pushes her hand through the wired greyness of the barrier. Emil's touch, however brief, makes her feel safe and desperate in the same moment. Many times since they were brought to the camp, she has considered the possibility of losing him. The reality of the danger they are in does not incite anger in her as much as it did in the beginning. She isn't as strong as she once thought she was, and she does not tell Emil that sometimes she simply wishes this was over, one way or another.

Their life together had been good, their work important. Then the pamphlets began circulating. The local television broadcasts had reported on the coming occupation. It was not something they took seriously, for it has happened before. The many natural resources in the region had always generated intense international interest. Despite the reports of the coming occupation and the building resistance, Talia and Emil had not believed it was possible that the world would allow this to happen. Even when the bombs finally fell, the moment did not seem real. Buena Gente was all but destroyed. Industrial areas were levelled and then occupied. Camps were set up. Anyone with ties to any political or military organization in Perda was gathered up by foreign soldiers and promised due process, but in the meantime, they would be held in temporary internment camps where they could be accounted for.

Talia and Emil had been taken the day of the first strikes. Pierre was with them, as he had been for weeks before the fighting began. After Buena Gente was hit, Pierre had gone straight away to his office for help. But the building had already been taken over. Talia, Emil and Pierre were taken into custody later that day.

Talia's family was taken too. They had arrived at the camp earlier on the same day when Talia, Emil and Pierre had arrived. Talia could not look at her mother when she first entered the tent that she was assigned to and saw that Bellona was standing there. Bellona was suddenly very little and powerless. She was no longer the leader of a rapidly and successfully developing country, but instead she was simply another caged animal. Bellona remained silent about their confinement. But Alberto was enraged, suspicious that Bellona, his wife whom he had loved for so long but no longer understood, had something to do with the camps. He was also worried for Talia. He had wept when he saw his daughter for the first time in many weeks because he was not happy to see her. He was distressed that she too would have to endure such betrayal and such a violation of her human rights.

The grounds were large and spread out over the rough landscape. Metal fences and gates had been erected alongside the entwined, thorny branches of the lower shrubbery that composed the camp's perimeter, forming a dual opportunity for physical mutilation for those who attempted escape. Inside the fences, the high grasses of the plains swayed in the wind that moved among close to fifty canvas tents. The grasses were not yet trampled by the repetitive footsteps of the interned. The camp was dissected into three parts, the areas divided by tall wire fences—their flat, grey patterns interrupted periodically by gates allowing passage between the segments of the grounds.

Six scaffolded towers marked exit and entry points to the camp. Armed guards manned each of the towers. A few buildings marked the northern end of the camp. One of the buildings, the barracks, housed the soldiers and served as their headquarters. The other two buildings housed lavatories. These buildings were separated by one of the wire fences, with a gate between them that remained open. The remaining space in these two enclosures was dotted with the large tents. The third fenced-off area, completely closed off to the camp's inhabitants, held military equipment and artillery.

At first, for the most part, the foreign soldiers had been benign. Food was adequate, and there were ample blankets and other linens supplied. The tents each housed three or four families. Talia was surprised when speaking to some of the residents of their tent. The others were not concerned with Talia or Bellona's presence—for they too came from high governmental or military positions. Bellona knew who most of them were but she did not speak to any of them, nor did they speak to her. They regarded Bellona with a sort of malice that Talia understood. When Talia talked to her mother about this, Bellona told her to keep quiet and not to speak to anyone about anything.

The captives were outraged, insulted and dubious because of the lack of response to their increasingly heated demands. Their strong reactions were not discouraged, nor were they met with threats of violence, and so the demands intensified. The soldiers promised information, but no explanations were offered. The washroom facilities had been adequately supplied. A laundry was run regularly.

Then the situation began to deteriorate. The inhabitants became more and more unsettled and the soldiers distanced themselves from their prisoners. Before long, the toilets became stopped up and overflowed. The filth was everywhere as it became necessary to urinate and defecate elsewhere on the grounds. Illnesses followed. The cold weather and the proximity of the prisoners resulted in the rapid spread of a dangerous respiratory illness, which began to take lives.

In the camp, there were women and men, and children clinging desperately to the adults they recognized, loved and looked to for answers. The adults instinctually and emotionally bound to protect them. Mothers could not pull their babies close enough, deeply into their breasts, into their hearts and away from this embryonic horror. The first to die were those who were already unwell, young children and the aged.

Pierre became sick soon after the outbreak, but he was strong and recovered quickly. Talia spent many hours considering their situation, discussing it with Emil and Pierre, waiting for sadness or terror to emerge in her heart and soul. But none of that happened. She marvelled that human beings could be such adaptable creatures. She accepted the new normal with little incredulity or emotional upheaval. They were prisoners of war, like so many that she had seen in images on television, like so many she had read about in history texts. She would not compare her fate and the fate of her family to the people in those situations.

Talia knew in her heart that the rest of the world was unaware of this camp's existence. And perhaps there were other camps just like this one in the Republic of Perda, where others were experiencing what she was. She began to feel the agony of dread taking hold of her.

One day, after many weeks in the camp, the soldiers were quiet. They did not do their usual rounds. Food was not provided, and the buzzing of the generators—barely audible most days—was the only constant sound carrying across the grounds. Those encamped knew something was wrong; they had developed a keen sense of danger and foreboding. They had become as well trained and sensitive as caged rats.

It was Alberto who first saw the tanks. Three of them approached from the east and more came from the opposite direction.

The shells were thunderous, and they immediately hit the guard towers, all six, practically simultaneously. The people in the camp did not scream or run, for this could be deliverance— perhaps they were saved. The first people at the gate waited to greet their saviours. The tanks emptied and their human cargo, all men, some wearing camouflage suits, others wearing what could have been everyday clothing, entered the gates shouting, or shooting at anyone who resembled a guard. These were not saviours after all: perhaps they were a newly formed militia, they were definitely unrecognisable. They swiftly infiltrated the camp, closing its gates behind them once again, and suddenly a fate more hideous than imaginable was a reality.

Talia and Emil huddled together in the tent with Bellona and Alberto. The others might have been screaming. There was certainly chaos, but the sound of Emil's breathing as he held her filled Talia's ears and her heart. Life as they had known it was over now. Their new life was baptized in violence—in her father's quiet death a few short moments later when a bullet pierced the inadequate canvas of the tent. The new soldiers were outside of the tent laughing and screaming at the interned as they scattered, terrified. This was the first indication of the callousness and cruelty these men were capable of.

Talia saw her father fall to the floor, her mother bent beside him screaming. Talia could do nothing but watch in disbelief. Her sense of loss wanted to pull her into madness, to a place from which she would never be retrieved. Emil did not move or speak. The shock had been too much for all of them.

A soldier entered the tent, before their disbelief could become grief, before Talia could place her hand upon her father for the last time. The soldier shouted and waved the muzzle of his gun toward a woman near the door. She fell to her knees submissively, begging for him to spare her life. He laughed at the woman after he lunged at her, causing her to flinch and hold her head protectively. Then the soldier looked over at Bellona as she hovered in grief over Alberto.

He approached Bellona, pushed her away from her husband's body, which was then removed roughly, with neither care nor sympathy. Talia watched everything without protesting, without defending her mother. All she could think about was her father. Every memory, every word of anger she had ever spoken toward him, every embrace, conversation, gift that he had ever given her, every kind word, every second of life with him flooded her mind with crippling intensity. Emil held her hand tightly, until his grip expressed his concern. Talia watched quietly knowing that any defiance would be futile and would result in more violence.

More soldiers then came into the tent shouting for the children to be gathered. Families were separated, as mothers begged for their children to remain with them. Men and women promised money, some offered themselves in place of their children. The children were taken from their parents, loaded into trucks as their relatives, and strangers alongside them watched impotently.

Talia's fingers are still entwined with Emil's. Now, weeks later, these new soldiers do not speak to the prisoners, except to shout instructions. They do not answer questions about the children they took, and they will strike, or worse, anyone who presses for more information. Emil's touch has pulled Talia back to the present. Her father's death was weeks ago and still she will not speak to Emil, or anyone, about it.

She looks away from Emil. He needs to see her strength, not her sadness or the pervasive sense of despair that stays with her now. She needs to show him that it is still within her to be strong.

§

Emil, Pierre, and Talia whisper cautiously behind one of the lavatory buildings in the camp. The water has been turned off. The toilets and showers are unusable. The stench would be unbearable if the interned had not grown accustomed to its constant company.

"I've tried to speak to them. The same guard is near our tent every morning. He says hello sometimes." Emil is hopeful, but these daily discussions seem pointless, and at the same time, absolutely necessary.

"Which one is he? I've never seen you speaking to one of them." Talia has developed her own theories about the camp, but she is keeping them to herself for the time being.

"I don't want him to see you with me. If he sees us together, he might recognize you."

"What if they have already recognized my mother and me, and they don't care? They are our militia, I'm sure of it. Their uniforms ... "

"Not all of them." Pierre leans back against the wall. "Some of them are occupying forces. Only some of them are ours. I don't think they know who we are. I don't think they give a shit. You look so different with your short hair, and I don't think they know you and your mother are here, or any of us for that matter." Pierre looks at Talia. She is still beautiful, despite the fatigue and malnourishment from which they are all suffering. Just over two months of little food and little water—Talia's face is drawn, her tall frame has become so thin that she leans forward constantly as though she is hollow. Talia's hair has been short since before the takeover of the camp, and its thick, auburn curls lie softly around her face. She and Bellona had cut their hair when they could not wash it any longer. Talia's eyes—deep blue-green and full of purpose and energy—are her only unchanged features.

Talia feels so dirty. They have not been able to clean their clothes other than airing them out every few days. Her fingernails are full of sand and soil, and her skin and hair has become soft and dull with the excess oil.

Talia's short hair makes her look young, uncomplicated. Pierre loves Talia. He has loved her for at least two years. But Emil has been his friend since childhood, and this is of equal importance. And Pierre's allegiance to Bellona has been sincere. Because of this allegiance, he could not be with Talia even if the opportunity presented itself. Talia has never been able to completely look past Pierre's role in her mother's administration. Talia loves Emil in any case. Pierre is sure of this. But this does not diminish his love for Talia.

"How can that be? Why would they do that ... join forces? It doesn't make sense. Someone else knew we were here and perhaps saw a strategic opportunity. Pierre, maybe they just want us to believe they are foreign." Emil is sceptical of Pierre's theories. Pierre is too suspicious at times, and immature, and this affects his judgment.

"Come on Emil. These buildings were here already. They must have been military training facilities or something. The facilities were here, and it is isolated. The occupying forces set up these camps to keep us in check. They underestimated the militia, and apparently some of their own ranks. And it doesn't matter how this began, but some of these new soldiers *are* foreign. I heard them speaking. I had already considered the possibility and then I heard a few of them talking last night." Pierre's ideas about the occupying forces changed the moment he too was interned. "How could you and my mother allow this to happen Pierre? How stupid to have trusted these people. You and my mother actually negotiated with them and, ha, what a joke ... they put you in here with rest of us! And now look where we are! They are using us! Don't you understand that?" Talia loses her temper, surprising herself as much as she does Pierre and Emil. Pierre just looks at her. Talia is dead right. He is shocked by the accuracy of her accusation, but he will die before he admits that what she believes is true. He hoped that Talia would not eventually turn on him because of his allegiance to Bellona. But he knew that she would. As much as he loves her, he won't allow her to condemn his principles and the good work that he has done. It was Bellona's decision to agree to the camps, not his and he won't be implicated because of Bellona's decision. He had no choice and the camps were supposed to protect as much as they were designed to isolate the politically connected members of Perda. His incarceration, and Bellona's, and the takeover of the camp—none of it could have been anticipated. But it should have been anticipated. Pierre is angry with Talia, or perhaps he is angry with himself. "You can be so damn rash sometimes Talia. You just open your mouth and you don't even think about what you are saying." Pierre exhales loudly and walks away. He hides his concern, but his need to protect her is transparent.

"Pierre, wait." Emil turns to Talia. "You need to be careful my love. We need one other in this." Emil chastises Talia and he walks away toward Pierre.

Talia knows that Pierre is keeping something from them. She wants him to be angry, so angry that he will admit whatever it is that he is hiding. Talia runs to catch up to Pierre and Emil.

"Wait. Pierre. Wait." She stops to catch her breath. "'I'm sorry. I'm just tired."

Emil sighs.

Pierre stops, but looks away from her. He knows things that Talia and Emil do not know. Things that he cannot share at this point, for he might lose them both. Besides, what does it matter any more how all of this came to be? It is something much bigger now, well outside of their control.

"Forget about it. All I care about is our safety. I would never do anything to jeopardize that. Talia, you and your mother do have to be careful about being recognized. You don't know what could happen."

"I still don't think they care, but regardless, my mother and I have been careful about being seen together. She has barely left the tent since my father's death. The others know who we are and have said nothing. They won't Pierre. Really. They would be in trouble too if they were recognized."

Emil speaks sharply. He raises his voice. "You're wrong." Talia's recklessness, the simplicity of her arguments—Emil worries about her all the time. "My love, you are underestimating yours and your mother's importance." Emil is very frustrated. "Goddamnit Talia, how many times do we have to do this? You *have* to be careful, you have to be smarter." Emil reaches out for her hand.

Talia is silent. She pulls her hand out of Emil's reach. It is rare that Emil raises his voice toward her. She simply nods.

Talia's expression leaves Pierre bewildered. He wants to take hold of her, to tell her how he feels and that he wants to protect her and love her. Instead, he agrees with Emil and tells Talia that she needs to be more careful in as steady a voice as he can manage.

Emil watches as her eyes seem to scour the trodden earth for some semblance of meaning in the events of the past weeks. Talia is different now—unravelled since her father's death. She is thin and always looks so tired. Her skin has grown pale and she appears small despite her height. She attempts to hide her sadness and her fear, but not well enough. Emil has tried to talk to her about her feelings. Her tenacity is one of the things he loves about her. But she will not accept help when she needs it and this is a dangerous aspect of her personality.

Talia looks at Emil. She is filled with resentment for her mother, because her mother's government created this instability, and allowed the ensuing occupation. She is worried for Emil. She dreads that their life together as they knew it is over, and that their country will be destroyed beyond restoration.

Emil ignores Talia's attempts to push him away. He pulls Talia toward him. Talia mildly protests but she moves toward Emil voluntarily.

Pierre looks away. After a moment, he interrupts. "I'm sure they have records, but they don't seem to care about our identities, at least not right now. Listen. There aren't enough of them. There are only two guards at the western gate during the night. We could get through, if we went at the right time."

"The western gate is beside the guards' barracks. This is crazy." Talia can't help but be pessimistic. "You cannot speak to anyone about this, Pierre, no one. Whatever we do, it can only be done by us. I will only tell my mother when we decide to go," Talia says, reaffirming her stance regarding Bellona. Talia is constantly aware of Pierre's past allegiance to Bellona.

"We don't know anything about this militia. The soldiers are unpredictable and violent." Emil says, imploring Talia to listen to him, but her determination is evident.

"We need to take advantage of—" The sound of gunfire interrupts Talia's voice.

Before they can determine the direction of the shots within the landscape of the larger battle, Talia is yanked down from behind. A soldier yells at her and pulls her away from Emil and Pierre. She is dragged by her hair and her clothing. Emil lunges for Talia, falls and crawls forward. He is grabbing her feet and calling her name. His powerlessness consumes him as the guns are pointed toward him. He looks at Talia's face. She shakes her head violently, begging him to be calm and to leave her. She screams, "Don't, don't!" Emil lets her go. The soldier ignores him, but might have shot him. Pierre helps Emil up and they watch Talia. She has been forced upright and she is walking alongside her captor. Pierre too is filled with horror. He is ashamed that during that brief struggle, he considered the possibility that if Emil were shot, he could be there for Talia. In that brief moment, an alternative reality was closer than ever.

Pierre watches, stunned as other women are gathered from the groups in which they were standing, pulled from tents, kicked and beaten, pushed roughly toward the place where Talia is now standing. She is already consoling the women crying beside her.

Emil is frantic. "They know who she is, Pierre, they'll kill her. Christ, they're going to kill her."

"Be calm, Emil. If they knew who she was, they would have taken us too. They are taking all the women ... look." Pierre points at the main group of women as they huddle together. The soldiers are shouting at them to move.

The women are strangely quiet as more join the expanding assembly. Emil keeps his eyes on Talia. She looks up at him, begging him silently to remain calm. Her arm is around the shoulders of the woman beside her.

"They're separating the men from the women." Emil watches as Talia disappears into the crowd of women. The soldiers herd them through one of the gates near the soldiers' barracks. The gate, between the two fenced-in areas, and which had remained opened, is closed behind them. It happens so fast.

One of the other men lunges desperately toward the gate. He is calling out for his loved one. He moves just a few feet forward before he is stopped abruptly. The bullets enter him. His cries are muffled as he falls to his knees, gurgling and spitting blood and saliva. He does not fall forwards or backward. Instead, his body slumps, leaning slightly to one side and his eyes are open and empty.

There is screaming and crying. Bullets are sprayed into the air as an additional warning. Emil and Pierre are down on the ground, Emil looks toward Talia and thinks of nothing else.

§

Talia and Emil meet each day on opposite sides of the fence that divides the men from the women. Talia's new normal is this: fingers entwined through a metal fence in a prison camp in a country that was once peaceful, beautiful and developing. Her ability to love has been corrupted by the hatred she feels toward those who have taken her freedom, her father, and her ideas about life away from her.

The separation of the men and the women didn't make sense at first. But news of attempted escapes moved rapidly through the camp. The men and women have been separated in order to divide families. Husbands will not leave without their wives or vice versa. This is what the soldiers believe. News has also spread about the soldiers' visits to the women's tents. Emil asks about this and Talia promises him that she has not been harmed or even touched by any of the soldiers. She does not tell Emil that just a few nights before she and Bellona had lain silently, listening to the cries of a woman not three feet away from them. Talia didn't move when the soldier finished, rose and exited the tent. Bellona had moved to console the woman, helping the woman to her bed and patting her back as though she was a child wakened by a nightmare. The gesture had stunned Talia, who had never felt her mother's arms around her in consolation. Emil does not need to know that this happened, and that it could have happened to Talia.

"We'll get through this." Emil always says this as he pulls his fingers away from hers and returns to the group of men.

Talia insists that they do not spend too much time speaking or touching, but that it is equally important that they speak and touch as often as they can. Daily if possible. They are not watched, nor do the guards even seem to care that many of the men and women meet at the fence each day.

Talia doesn't know how to feel about living, but she lives for Emil. She even lives for her mother. She wants to live, but not this way, constantly threatened with the loss of her own life or the loss of Emil's or her mother's life.

Emil smiles at her as he walks away. She feels the same crippling sadness that she felt when she watched her father's lifeless form being dragged away.

Talia feels more than panicked when Emil leaves her to return to life on his side of the hideous barrier. Remorse and guilt engulf her when she remembers the one and only moment in time in which she was unfaithful to Emil. She knows it wasn't her fault, because she had not anticipated the kiss. But she hadn't refused to accept the unexpected embrace. She was confused afterwards, angry because she *had* felt something she didn't want to feel. In addition to this betrayal, she had lied to Emil when, later that day, he had asked her why she was so upset. She will never tell him about Pierre. She won't speak of it to anyone. All that matters is that they live and that Emil knows how much she loves him.

§

Alberto Adalardo turns in response to his daughter's defiance. "You should not have gone. There is nothing else to talk about, Talia. You always do what you want to do!" Alberto loves his daughter. He is immensely proud of her, but her insubordination is incorrigible.

"That isn't true, and it's unfair. I do what I believe is right because that is what you've taught me to do. I didn't go to the rally to shame you or Mother." Talia knows that her father agrees with her, even though he will never admit it openly. Talia sees hope in her father's expression—hope that she won't be deterred by his obligatory response to her participation in the campaign for reform.

"You knew the damage it would cause. There is nothing else to say now—it's done. You don't even know why you are doing this Talia."

"There *are* things to say, Papa! But you have no interest in hearing my opinion or any opinion other than Mother's. There is just as much wrong in that. And don't tell me that I don't know why I'm doing this. *You* aren't doing anything!" Talia turns away from her father. She holds back her tears as heat rises to her cheeks. Her ears are warm to the touch as she brushes her loose hair behind them. Her father's disappointment is unbearable. "I *believe* in what I am doing Papa. We don't want violence that is avoidable. We are making important contacts in the world and we are keeping them informed. They don't know the truth about the occupation. We need to stop it before it begins. We make phone calls, we write letters, and we protest, peacefully. That's all. Tell me, *why* is this wrong? My own *mother* is sponsoring the destruction of our country. My God, why can't you understand that I *have* to do something about that?"

"Talia, enough!" Alberto raises his hand to strike her. She shifts backward a step, but he lowers his hand. He hangs his head. He turns away from her.

"I'm sorry, Papa, but only for hurting you." Talia cannot look at him as she begins to walk out of the room. She knows his face will be drawn with resignation.

She turns to acknowledge her father before leaving the room. He is not looking at her, but stands facing the window. His arms are folded across his chest and his broad and strong back expands and contracts as he sighs.

Sadness engulfs her.

Talia goes to her bedroom, closes the door behind her. She should feel something about betraying her parents' wishes, but her conviction is directed elsewhere. It is deeper and stronger than the resentment she feels toward them.

Perda will be destroyed if this occupation is allowed to take place. The young people of Perda are more cynical, more disturbed than the generations before them. The young people have learned disparagement, and to expect dishonesty. Suspicion is epidemic amongst her peers and her parents will never understand. She is not a child, and she is far from under the thumb of her family's political obligations, despite her mother's insistence that the reformists are paranoid. Talia believes that the reformists' fears are accurate and grounded in the reality of the situation. According to her mother, what Talia has already done is tantamount to treason. Bellona doesn't know yet that Talia has now agreed to lead the campaign for reform.

It is time to leave her family's home, despite being unmarried. She does not wish for marriage, nor does she fear life outside her family's money and circle of influence. What she fears is the future and the self-destructive path her country's politicians have embarked upon. The people of Perda will not be oppressed, nor will they become slaves to a foreign entity's economic ambitions, no matter how beneficial it might appear to be in the short term.

Emil is right. Talia knows he is right. She should have left years ago, but she wanted every bit of the education to which her family's status entitled her. Hypocrisy or not, she wasn't forgoing the opportunity to attend one of the best universities in the world. Emil understood; he always understood. After all, he had made the same choice that she had. He often looks at her apologetically when they discuss her family before taking her face in his hands.

Talia loves her parents. She is devoted to Emil and she is loyal to her country. Her feelings for all of them overwhelm her with their complexity. She brought Emil into this fight, although it was he who inspired her rebellion in the first place. He encouraged her to listen to her instincts, despite her family connections. He trusts her implicitly, this she knows implicitly. He will always do what is right, and he defines right and wrong for himself as she does.

Emil should be on his way to meet her at the market, as they had planned at the rally. The rally had not been much of anything after all, but cameras were ever-present at such events and Talia's attendance always noted. Her mother's position in the government brings Talia the publicity she needs in order to propagate the ideals of the campaign for reform. And now that they have asked her to lead the reform group, there is no turning back.

This time Talia has intentionally forced her mother's hand and she feels a deep sense of relief.

§

Emil watches Talia as she approaches the market throughway that runs between the market stalls. Emil wishes that Talia would not suggest meeting in open places like this without protection. But she insists that it is safer to meet in public, and that she won't be followed constantly by an entourage the way her mother is.

The late-afternoon heat lifts smells from the vendors' stalls and circulates the odours around the shoppers as they browse and quibble. The anglers' stalls produce the most pungent odours and Talia's face turns away from their smells as she passes them hurriedly, heading toward the place where Emil is waiting for her.

She smiles as she nears him. Her eyes are weary and her rubbing of them has produced red and slightly swollen ridges under her eyelashes.

She reaches for Emil, pulls him close, and embraces him emphatically. Emil gently pushes her away and asks if her parents have confronted her yet. Talia shakes her head and simply says she does not want to go over it again.

Emil smiles slightly and fixes his eyes on Talia. She meets his smile with a smirk and her uneasiness seems to dissolve, as it usually does when they are together. Emil watches her demeanour change simply because she is with him. She relaxes and becomes playful, sensuous and flirtatious. She exudes a confidence that he has always found irresistible. He's had girlfriends, relationships that were founded on intellect, admiration or physical attraction. His relationship with Talia is very different though. He has watched her grow, from a time when they were both just children, into a young woman full of curiosity and passion. He knew he loved her years ago, but he wonders if he hasn't always loved her. The age difference is not significant now, but when she was fifteen and he was twenty-three, it was significant enough to discourage him from being with her. Her father would never have allowed it, and probably doesn't approve as it is. Emil doesn't care. He has tried, without success, to win over Talia's father, and he knows that Talia has long since given up on seeking her father's approval when it comes to her relationship with Emil. Still, they keep their connection hidden as much as possible, for many reasons, not the least of which is Emil's intrinsic involvement in Talia's campaign against her mother's government.

Bellona Adalardo is an intelligent woman. Talia's confidence is, without question, due to her mother's example. But Bellona's pride prevents her from accepting her recent failures as a politician. Bellona's pride has alienated her daughter and her husband, but Bellona seems to be as oblivious to their alienation as she is to her own diminishing career. If Bellona is faced with any physical evidence of Emil's involvement in the campaign for reform, she will ruin him, and it would be easy for her to do this. Emil is not gullible enough to think that Bellona would spare him because of his relationship with Talia. In fact, his relationship with Talia is a liability as far as Bellona is concerned. Emil's parents are political exiles, although many years ago, his family was very close to Talia's. Emil has not spoken to his own parents or siblings for years because of his choice to remain involved with Talia.

"What are you thinking about?" Talia takes his hand and shakes it lightly.

"Your mother. I wish it wasn't so hard for you."

"If it wasn't this way, I wouldn't be who I am. My mother has good qualities, but she also has dangerous ideas. I inherited some of those qualities, along with my father's idealism. I think it is what you find so attractive about me, that I am so young and malleable, ha!" She pokes at Emil's side and pulls him along toward a colourful display of fresh produce and flowers. She picks up an eggplant and looks at it thoughtfully.

"You amaze me," he says. "Just the way you look at the world, at things ... "

"It's just an eggplant, Emil. You're too serious. I've had enough of serious today." She jabs at him again.

Emil picks up a basket and carries it behind Talia as she chooses her items. He *is* too serious, but he knows that she also loves that he is serious. She has helped him to be more serious about the important things in their lives and he in turn has helped her to see that, like her mother, she is a born leader and she is more capable of inspiring the people of Perda than anyone else.

§

Sophie awakens to moonlit surroundings. She looks for Emil. He has fallen asleep a few feet away from her. The nausea has subsided and her head is no longer pounding as it had been. She pulls at her long, thick ponytail and removes the elastic holding it in place. Her dark hair falls against her shoulders, and the spot aches where her hair had been tied back. It is such a normal sensation. It seems completely out of place in the darkness of her current situation.

Sophie crawls across to Emil and places her hand on his forearm. "Emil."

He is startled and abruptly clasps her wrist. Emil looks at Sophie as she gasps and pulls her hand free.

He sits up. "I'm sorry. I forgot where I was."

"Emil. I have some questions." Sophie is tired and hungry, and unwilling to buffer her anxiety any longer.

"You're feeling better I guess." Emil's face is more visible in the nebulous surroundings.

"I want to know what we are going to do out here and why you won't let me return to the city. I was safe there until today. For all I know, nothing has happened to the hotel and you have taken me hostage. I want to go back. You destroyed the only means of transportation that we had—I just don't understand."

Emil shakes his head. "Sophie, I didn't plan this. You can do whatever you would like, but you'll be picked up before you get anywhere near the city again. A foreign journalist would be very valuable to any one of the factions." He is exhausted and exasperated with Sophie's insistence that they return to the city. She doesn't understand, or perhaps she won't accept, just how much trouble they are in.

"My father's parents were born here Emil. I was very close to them. It is the reason I requested this assignment." Sophie is proud to tell Emil that she has such a connection to Perda. He is not taking her seriously; she knows she is young, but she wants Emil to listen to her.

He is listening, but he conceals his reaction to this news. Emil has lost so many people. He doesn't want to like Sophie, to feel close to her. He is afraid of endangering another person that he cares about.

Sophie tries once again to get information from him. "Why were you hiding in the city?"

"I was a prisoner ... I escaped. My family didn't."

Emil is guarding the changes in his expression, but Sophie hears the shift in his voice. Under usual circumstances, her compassion would have vetoed her need for information. She presses on despite Emil's quiet tone. "Where is your family now?"

"I don't know. I'm not sure where anyone I used to know is. I've always lived here. I have friends here. I went to school here. But I have not seen a face that I recognize since the camp."

Sophie can't believe that Emil was encamped. The internment camps have been inaccessible to journalists, but rumours of their existence have fuelled a great deal of interest in international media outlets not outlined in the boycott.

Details about the suspected internment camps run by the occupying forces started circulating months ago, yet no intervention has been sanctioned with regard to the camps. All of this despite the claim that the foreign occupation is primarily a liberation operation. The occupying forces have denied the existence of these camps.

Nothing makes sense here. Once she arrived and met with the people of this country, Sophie no longer believed that the global community would permit this invasion to take place. She was wrong. It has been allowed to happen. It *is* being allowed to happen. And similar ambitions have been carried out throughout modern history. Sophie believes that the camps were planned secretly, and that they are an obvious ploy to undermine rebellion against the occupation. And yet no one has acted because of their rumoured existence.

"Emil, I'm sorry. I didn't know. How could you have ended up in a camp?"

"We were taken to the camp without warning by occupying forces soldiers. It seemed that all the prisoners were from political or military backgrounds. Then after many weeks, the camp was overtaken by an unknown faction. The children were removed; we don't know where they were taken. The men and women were then separated. The women were ... " Emil lifts one of the bottled waters they had taken from the truck to his lips. Without the sun's radiation, the air temperature has dropped dramatically.

He offers the bottle to Sophie and as she reaches forward, her hand and forearm are shaking involuntarily. She takes the bottle and drinks until it is empty. She is cold and uncertain, but she is no longer concerned about Emil's motivations.

"I know about the camps Emil. I mean, I've heard things about them, but nothing concrete. Was Talia Adalardo was among the interned? God, it doesn't make sense."

He does not answer, but Sophie hears his muted stubborn grunts, which she assumes are his attempts to regain his composure as he lifts himself from where he is sitting.

"We can see a bit better in this light. We need to keep moving, we've been here too long. If you feel sick again, we'll stop for another rest."

"I feel better now. I just need to go to the bathroom."

"Just go, it isn't safe to wander alone, even if it is just a small distance."

"Thank you for helping me, Emil. Thank you for getting me out of there."

Sophie slips behind some trees. When she is finished, she returns to where Emil is waiting. "I'm ready."

"Would you mind carrying the bag?"

"Of course not. Here, give it to me." Sophie reaches for the bag.

They walk in the dark.

§

The forest opens up and they are surrounded by the enormous trunks of ancient trees. The terrain is less difficult to negotiate. The ground is soft and littered with vines, roots and varied detritus. The trees are far enough apart, that Sophie is no longer concerned with losing sight of Emil as he moves ahead. Despite the absurdity of it, she is frightened of the animals that might be watching, perhaps even stalking them as they progress. She asks Emil if there are animals to be wary of and he says there are many creatures that could be dangerous, including large cats, snakes and certain insects. Sophie wishes that she had not asked.

Emil listens to and tries to answer Sophie's questions about the forest. He has been watchful all along for animals and insects in the trees. They have no medical supplies and a bite from any one of several creatures in the area could be fatal. It is a problem they don't need on top of what they are already dealing with. Sophie is walking more carefully now, and though Emil wants to cover ground as quickly as possible, he feels that her caution is appropriate.

Branches hang protectively and high above them. The canopy shifts constantly in the cool night wind. The fully risen moon shines down on top of them, brightening the surroundings significantly. The sound of the wind in the trees is very much like that of waves coming onto a sandy shore. This is the coldest it will become, and it is cold enough. Sophie is thankful that they are not in the more northern part of the country.

They are walking side by side now, as the trees are much further apart here. Sophie has picked up a twig from the ground. She absent-mindedly twists and pulls at it as she walks. "Emil, did you stay in the city to wait for Talia?" Sophie knows Emil is reluctant to discuss Talia, but she is sure that something has happened, something terrible, and she wants to know, to understand, what it means for the future of this conflict.

Emil has been worn down. "The building I was in, it was where we had lived together with a good friend of ours before we were taken to the camp." Emil clears his throat and is quiet for a moment. And then he continues. "After I got away, I thought I would find help in Buena Gente, or that Talia would look for me there if she somehow escaped."

"Talia *was* held in the camp with you? Why?"

"I don't know. The others in the camp were from political families also, or military families. I'm not sure. Talia believed that the camp was organized by the occupying forces to control us. I agreed with her, so did Pierre. Then the camp was taken over by the militia. I escaped, Talia didn't. Pierre was killed. That was a few days ago." Emil looks sideways at Sophie in a way that suggests he is finished with her questions.

"Emil, I want to respect your privacy. I do respect it. But you have my life in your hands. I'd like to know more. I need to know what will happen when we get to the border. I don't have any papers with me, no identification. And the camp, it just doesn't make sense to me that you and Talia were held. How do you expect me to accept that without more information?"

Emil doesn't want to feel angry with Sophie, but he feels agitated by her constant questions because these new questions are the questions of a reporter. He isn't willing to participate in the shifting direction of the rhetoric between them. "They'll know who you are at the border. They'll know who we both are. You know Sophie, whether you *accept* it or not doesn't really matter. No one knows what is happening in Perda. You've been here for what, a few weeks? Don't you question material when it falls in your lap? Or if the story is good, I suppose you don't bother asking yourself why the information was sent to you in the first place?"

Emil is right. She was ecstatic when the offer was presented. A fully paid adventure in a country on the brink of salvation, to be delivered from itself, from its forecasted economic catastrophe, by the means of targeted bombs and reconstructing the government. Sophie believed that her network was one of the good ones. That they wanted to tell the truth. She was told that Perda is to be controlled economically and politically from abroad, its resources handled by a group of allegedly well-intentioned first world nations—the Coalition of Nation for the Occupation of Perda. Very soon after her arrival in Perda, Sophie realized that everything the network told her was fabricated or perverted in some way. She had promptly quit and decided to stay on a freelance basis. There is nothing liberating about this invasion. It is oppressive in the least, its motivations surreptitious and falsely justified. Sophie sees hypocrisy in all aspects of the occupation, even the name given to the Coalition is hypocritical.

Sophie was too wrapped up in the opportunity. She had begged for it. She had taken advantage of the situation believing that she would not be influenced away from the truth. She knew that even if her benefactors had questionable motives, she could expose them at will if the evidence presented itself. She was intuitive and idealistic, and proud of both these defining characteristics. But they held her back almost as much as they allowed her insight. She saw situations, even horrific situations, as hopeful and full of potential. At least she had before watching this war develop and witnessing the subsequent destruction of entire families. The number of civilian losses thus far is astounding, and yet these losses are transparent in the eyes of the global community it seems. It has become Sophie's personal directive to record these losses above all else.

Her grandparents died some time ago and she feels nothing of them in the country where they were born, and where they lived most of their lives. Perda—centuries in the making—has been irrevocably damaged in a matter of weeks, and the systematic occupation has just begun.

Emil and Sophie come upon an open field. They move alongside its perimeter marked by grasses rising and swaying as high as Sophie's hips.

The area is uncomfortably exposed. "We should get down, Emil."

He crouches down, as she does.

"It's just farms and forest out here. Very little military presence in this territory, it's too far from the city centres and the terrain is too difficult to get vehicles through."

"What if we are seen? What if someone reports us?"

"It's safer here than in the city now. You would be a target there. You can't go back, Sophie. I can't go back either. It was difficult enough getting in before. It will be worse than ever.

There are checkpoints all around Buena Gente. If you had been in your hotel yesterday, you would have been killed."

"I wanted to come here to witness a great deliverance. To be like the journalists in flack jackets reporting from war zones around the world that I grew up admiring. But I'm not like them. I was so stupid and gullible."

"Many Perdans welcomed this occupation. They'll profit from this country's reconstruction, as will foreign companies. None of us really knew what would happen, not you, not me, none of us." Emil pauses. "We should keep walking around the field, not through it. There isn't enough cover and there will be snakes in those grasses." Emil extends his arm and points as he speaks, outlining the edges of the field before them.

The field is visible because it is the only area not covered in dense forest. Tall, dry, yellow-green stalks stretch as far as Sophie can see in the moonlight; the field has not been cultivated for some time. In the distance is a grouping of dark shapes ... houses or farm buildings perhaps. At the edge of the field the forest is dark and full of the sounds of nocturnal animal life—the voices, cries, songs, squeals of creatures unknown and the smell of green vegetation, dry wood and the sweet smell of beech trees permeates the air.

Sophie follows Emil as he walks between the trees, on the edge of the grassland. She understands now that he is helping her only because he has to. Because he is a good man.

She doesn't resent Emil's attitude toward her. She is ashamed of her misguided self-righteousness, even though she believed in the beginning that her self-awareness would protect her from contributing propaganda. She hasn't avoided this after all. Other journalists refused to come here altogether. They were probably right for doing so. Maybe not.

Emil sees that Sophie's conscience is good. He believes that she is beginning to understand the situation. She is as he and Talia were years ago, when they became more involved in the issues facing their society. Before that, they both had believed what they were taught, told, and raised to believe. Neither Emil nor Talia had truly questioned their own beliefs until Bellona's party was elected. That was years ago. During Bellona's term as the head of state in Perda, the Republic's culture, economy and people have been given over, deliberately and quietly, to international influence and control. All in preparation for this occupation—that in reality has, ironically, resulted in Bellona's descent from power.

Emil and Sophie approach the far end of the field where a few small buildings are visible. The closest structure appears to be a house. Its windows are dark but Emil says that they will not know if it is truly deserted until daylight. They should wait where they are until morning.

§

Bellona Adalardo hasn't wept in a long time. She cries this night with the fervour of a child. She cries for her daughter. Talia is headstrong, but so much like her father too. Bellona cannot tolerate any more of Talia's defiance, even if it means disowning her. The administration is toppling; Bellona knows this too well. She also knows that her daughter is closer to the truth than she realizes. Bellona's reluctance to acknowledge Talia's dissent is as much to protect Talia, as it is to preserve her position while the eyes of the world are upon her.

Despite Bellona's attempts to conceal the truth, Talia is determined to put things together accurately. Her campaigns against the proposed foreign military occupations endanger the security of the family. And now, Talia leading the reformists. Bellona won't have it.

Alberto is quiet when he enters the room, and Bellona is startled when he places his hand on her shoulder. She turns to him, postured stiffly. She wipes away her tears and lifts her hand to halt his defence of Talia before he utters even a word.

"Alberto, enough now. She is an adult for God's sake, a grown woman, and she lives in our *home!* She cannot live here, on our money, using our contacts, and then humiliate me publicly. My politics aside, I am her mother and her actions have endangered our family."

"Yes. Yes. I was not going to defend Talia this time. I agree with you. But, endangered? That is a little strong, don't you

THE BEAUTY OF THE WORLD

think? After all, it is precisely the use of that type of language and its implications that Talia protests."

"Things aren't good, Alberto, and my position will not help any of us now, especially with Talia constantly defying me in public. Don't you think they see this? I can't control my own daughter! This occupation is going to happen. Talia's involvement in these protests is suspicious. We will be affected as a family and I will not allow it any longer, nor should you."

"Bellona, you will not push her away any more than you already have. You are not the only person in this family!" Alberto's voice rises uncharacteristically. "Have you ever questioned your own politics? Haven't you considered the possibility that you are wrong? Maybe you have *always* been wrong about this. These things will happen. It's not within our control. We are headed toward a war, and they will take over. You can't believe otherwise. We have always known this was a possibility and yet, you still created this agreement and your administration went ahead with it. The Coalition will protect its interests before anything else. *You* are nothing in this." Alberto's voice has grown hoarse with emotion. He shakes his head. He steps aside for her as she moves past him without responding to his indictment of her government.

Bellona sits on the edge of the bed. She lifts her hairbrush from the night table and she thoughtfully turns it over and over in her hand. Her black hair falls across her shoulders, large curls spilling down her back like dark, heavy vines crawling toward the earth. She replaces the hairbrush without using it. Bellona rises and pulls on her robe over her night clothes. She leaves the room as Alberto sighs walking into the bedroom closet for his nightshirt.

Bellona makes her way down the stairs and past the adobe foyer to Talia's bedroom. She knocks on Talia's door. Talia does not answer. Bellona opens the door, enters Talia's room and closes the door behind her. She turns on the light and sees that Talia is sitting on the edge of her bed, unsurprised.

"What do you want?"

"Don't speak to me in that tone Talia. Your anger is no match for mine tonight! You have behaved like a child. A child! A spoiled child with no brain of her own, rebelling against the family that made you who you are. You don't know what is happening, you do not know what you are doing!" Bellona slams her hand against the surface of the bureau beside her. "Do you understand me?"

Talia is shaken by her mother's resentful tone, but she will not react. "Yes, I hear you, Mother, but I disagree."

Talia's calm defiance is too much. Bellona can only protect her family and her career if Talia is managed.

"I don't want you in this house any more, Talia. You will no longer have access to our money. The damage that you have inflicted on this family and on your country ... I'm ashamed to be your mother." Bellona is breathing heavily. She stops and inhales slowly to calm herself. "You are so damn selfish, armed with a little bit of knowledge. Do you really believe what you spew to the cameras? You will leave this house tomorrow."

Talia stares insolently at her mother. "I'm leaving tonight."

Talia is prepared to go and Bellona is not surprised. Bellona meets her daughter's glare with an over-eager stare, silently begging her only child to reconsider, to conform, for her safety and for the safety of their family.

Talia lifts a large bag from her closet—she has been ready for this moment for weeks. She stops in front of Bellona, who has tears streaming down her flushed cheeks, her dark eyes fixed on her daughter. Talia kisses Bellona on one cheek and then on the other. "You are no longer my mother."

This last statement pierces Bellona. She knows Talia is angry … just angry. She wants to turn, to pull Talia back into her arms. In the same moment, she wants to injure Talia as desperately as she has been injured.

§

"Talia, what's the matter? Why are you here?"

"I left. It's done. Now we can be together. Now we can make a real difference, Emil."

Her voice is smooth, her demeanour calm, but he knows Talia is broken. He has watched it happening. No matter how much she insists it is what she wants, Talia loves her mother. She has modelled herself after Bellona Adalardo. Talia is even stronger, but at times more careless than her mother. Emil worries about her. Always, he worries about her.

"I'm sorry, my love. I'm sorry." He holds Talia.

"I told her she is no longer my mother," Talia whispers. She needed to hurt Bellona for everything she felt Bellona had neglected to do in their relationship.

Emil consoles her. "She knows you love her."

Emil slips Talia's coat from her shoulders. He asks her to take off her shoes and clothes and he pulls her close to him in his bed. He holds her and smooths her hair away from her face. "Sleep. We'll talk tomorrow."

She nods and kisses him softly. Her face is warm and wet, but he does not comment on her tears.

§

Sophie eagerly awaits their next movement. She is quiet though, and she and Emil have barely spoken since they settled at the edge of the field waiting until morning. They are caught between a city in ruin and unfriendly terrain, without food and with little to no protection.

Emil is also awake, and thinking. Sophie is headstrong and kind, and too much like Talia. The constant reminder of Talia's uncertain fate is almost unbearable.

"We should leave for the house." Sophie is cold, the chill has seeped into her bones over the last many hours of darkness. She is underdressed in just jeans, an oxford shirt and a sweater, but thankful that the air is dry and not damp. She has not seen any movement anywhere.

"The house is empty. I've been watching." Emil stands and brushes sand away from his clothing. The edge of the field is soft and dry where it joins the forest. The region is unlike any other in the country on the edge of all climates. This fertile agricultural land is situated at the base of the foothills. The foothills lead into the mountains, which descend on the other side into a desert that stretches into other lands. Perda is surrounded by mountains and desert and at any given moment, meteorological contradictions are occurring somewhere within its borders.

Emil once tried to convince Talia that they should leave the city, their old lives, and become farmers. They would have a small home, children and an idyllic existence. Talia opposed the idea.

She said Emil's romantic expectations would never be fulfilled and that she did not want to disappoint him. Emil closes his eyes for a moment and he imagines Talia lying beside him.

§

Sophie and Emil are almost at the small house. The surroundings are completely deserted. As they near the dwelling, Sophie can see that a portion of the house's exterior has been burned. Otherwise, it is pastoral and small, and apparently constructed from natural materials. It looks as though it has been abandoned for many years—not just since the months since the war began. The house is surrounded with tall grasses and trees with vines that hang intimately about their trunks. The vines are a rich brown, not very different from the colour of the tree trunk but for tiny red flowers, that give the illusion that the trunk has been stung by a thousand insects and it is now bleeding from its tiny wounds. The flowers seem out of place.

The beauty of the landscape is strange against the broken world around it. The house is made from wood with sand and clay rubbed against it. Emil explains that this is a traditional native home and that the clay is meant to keep out animals, insects and to absorb moisture. The burned portion is closest to the roof, where a controlled fire within might have escaped into the night via the vent in the roof and lit that portion on fire also. The hole burned in the roof is not large.

Emil pushes against the front door. It gives easily and they enter the home. Thick dust hangs in the air, suspended as though each particle is laced with light. The air smells of rotten foodstuffs and must.

The house is divided into two rooms. The main space contains a table with simple wooden chairs, and shelves built into the walls are lined with cooking utensils, pots and glass jars. A crude pump sink is centred against the back wall.

Emil walks over to the sink and he lifts the pump's handle repeatedly. It has rusted badly. "We'll have to get water from the river."

Sophie enters the other room. A wooden slatted bed frame leans against the wall. There is no mattress. A small window looks out onto a fenced area that contains wildly grown plants. Perhaps it was once a garden.

Sophie is suddenly overwhelmed. Her legs begin to tremble beneath her and she feels her throat constricting. She leans over and allows her head to hang.

"Are you all right?"

Sophie cannot look up at Emil. She feels weak but also compelled to try to remain composed. Her body betrays her. She slips to her knees and begins to cry. She can't hold back the sobs and soon she is sucking intermittent breaths like a distraught child.

Emil approaches her. He squats beside her.

"I'm afraid, Emil. I'm afraid of what will happen. I see Tom's face over and over, and I think of his wife and his children and I imagine them telling her ... " Sophie stops. She wipes her face and she looks straight at Emil. "I don't think I can handle this."

Emil understands Sophie's fear and her desperation, but he can feel nothing for anyone, including himself until he knows something of Talia. He does not speak. A forced sympathetic overture is not something he can accomplish. He too is emotionally and physically exhausted. Months of malnourishment and worry in the camp have left him weakened and without stamina. Knowing that Talia remains in the camp keeps him focused and thinking only of her.

The house on the farmland will suffice temporarily. The border is still a good distance from this farm. The journey will be partially through the mountains and the going will be difficult without supplies. The mountains are sparsely occupied, mostly by isolated villages, but the border may be guarded.

Sophie's tears are justified. They have much to go through yet.

"Don't apologize." Emil rests a hand on Sophie's back.

§

"What have you done?" Alberto's voice sounds weary as he comes into the bedroom from the adjoining bathroom.

"I did what was best for us, and for Talia." Bellona rises from the edge of the bed where she was sitting, waiting for him. She walks to him and stands close. She is seething. "You will not speak to me in that tone of voice. She is my daughter too and she has betrayed us, again and again. Talia is young and foolish and she has put us all in danger. I made a choice that you are not man enough to make." When Bellona starts to walk past him, Alberto catches her wrist and twists it slightly, enough to ignite a small throbbing pain in the palm of her hand.

"You've done this alone Bellona. It was always you and your career. Nothing in this family has ever been decided without first considering its effect on your career. You have betrayed your family and your country, not Talia. And you know it." Alberto releases Bellona's wrist and sits on the bed. He is turned sideways and staring forward.

Bellona looks at her husband with his hands in fists as he sits quietly reconciling his failed relationships. Alberto has spoken a truth that Bellona had not believed he was capable of bringing to her. His words are stark, fierce, and disarming.

He loved her once. He supported her education and her rise in politics. *She* has failed. No one else. She is all but powerless and this truth will soon be revealed to the entire country, to the world. Everything she worked toward is collapsing. Her administration has mishandled every aspect of the resources trade agreement and without the power they once had, the occupation has become less and less voluntary. She is a liability now, a reminder of a great failure. She is of no importance to the foreign companies that now own large portions of Perda's territory. Her daughter's involvement in the campaign for reform has demonstrated that the Adalardo family is publicly unstable and disloyal. The war will come soon and Bellona will not end her career this way. She tells herself that it will be all right. That she has many powerful friends, friends that she has quietly, significantly remunerated for their support of her recent policies. The Coalition of Nations for the Occupation of Perda will protect the Republic and her administration's beliefs in the country's economic future. One day, she hopes, Perdans will look back and see her as a critically important and brave leader.

§

Emil awakens, realizes the telephone is ringing. Talia's breathing is quick and her sleep fitful. She has all but pulled the blankets off the bed. He turns his back to her as he removes the telephone from its cradle.

"Hello ... this is Emil."

"Emil, this is Alberto Adalardo."

"Mr. Adalardo ... it's very late."

"I know. I just want to know if Talia is with you."

"She is."

"I'd like to speak to my daughter please, Emil."

"I'm sorry, sir, but she is—"

"Let me speak." Talia places her hand on Emil's back.

Emil holds the phone over his shoulder for her to take from him. He listens intently, lying on his side, his back to her.

"Papa?" Talia holds her hand against Emil's back. "I know you're worried, but I'm fine ... Well, Mother will say what she needs to in order to convince you that I'm wrong ... If you didn't want to hear this, you shouldn't have called here. I love you, Papa. I love both of you ... I know you understand ... No, Papa, *this* is what needs to be done and it could not be done any more with me living at home. I should have left sooner, before it came to this ... That isn't true ... No, Papa ... Goodbye, Papa."

Talia hands the phone over Emil's shoulder and he replaces it in the cradle.

"I'm sorry, my love. For all of this." She presses her face against his back.

He turns over to face her. "I have never asked you to be sorry for anything. Now's the time to become stronger, not to make apologies. We will get through all of these troubles."

"I know we will. I know what we are capable of."

"Talia, you have to listen to me. You will be targeted soon, if you haven't been already. We need to be careful now. We need to know what they are planning. Not just your mother, but also the occupying forces. We should meet with Pierre tomorrow."

"I am not afraid of my mother's friends, Emil."

"There are more influences involved in this, Talia, than just your mother's friends. You're stubborn, and it's not a time to be careless."

"I'm being careful. I'm always careful. If not for my own sake, for yours ... I'm tired, I want to sleep now. We'll meet with Pierre tomorrow and we'll find out what he knows. But I can't go with you if you meet him at the Capital Building. My mother can't see me, and she cannot see you with Pierre either. You should ask him to meet you away from the building."

"Of course, but I want you to come with me. You can wait elsewhere while I speak to him. But we should stay together. Now go back to sleep."

Emil kisses Talia. She smells of perfume and of sweat.

§

It is a night of confusion. Never before has she questioned her ideals, her motives. Bellona had risen so easily within the government, aided considerably by her father's reputation as a fair and just man and a decorated war hero. Despite her father's role in her initial hiring, Bellona has worked to make a name for herself as an individual in the government. She is intelligent and she is ambitious, as her father was.

This night she has acted not with her mind but with her heart. She has behaved rashly, out of a want for control instead of good judgment. Now Talia will not return and her safety is more compromised than before. This isn't what Bellona had hoped for.

Talia is headstrong and she does not consider her own need for protection. Bellona knows what she has to do and she will do it. The plans for the internment camps are already underway and Bellona believes they are necessary, for now. The camps will keep the interned safer than they will be anywhere else once the inevitable fighting begins. She will visit the camps personally; her role by then will be reduced to spokesperson for the government. Her visits will make the interned feel important, protected. They will understand that this is for the ultimate good of the Republic. To keep those with obvious political leanings against the coming occupation from causing more turmoil than is necessary. Bellona will continue to placate the emissaries of the occupying forces, who hold all the power as they maintain their agendas privately and publicly.

Bellona waits for her husband to return home. He has been gone for over an hour, she doesn't know where. When he comes through the door, Bellona is surprised. She thought briefly that he might not return, and yet she knows he would never leave his family, even though she has pushed him close to leaving many times. She is seated on the arm of a high backed chair, in the dimly lit warmth of the library they have so carefully assembled over the years. Bellona always does her thinking at home in the library, surrounded by its dark shelves filled from floor to ceiling with volumes. Bellona feels safe in this room, untouchable.

"Alberto ..." Bellona remains seated.

Alberto enters the library. He stops in front of her. "Bellona, I don't want to speak to you any more tonight."

"Alberto, please."

She stops him by placing her hand in his as he goes to leave. He does not pull away. Instead, his large, calloused palm accepts her grasp. Perhaps soon he will accept her apology too.

"I was wrong, Alberto. I have been wrong for a long time, I know I have been." Bellona has to make him believe that he can trust her again. She has to convince him that he can let her deal with Talia, without questions.

Alberto turns to Bellona and kneels beside her.

"Bellona, you have changed so much. Talia is gone because of you. My daughter is in danger now, because of you."

"*Our* daughter, and yes, I told Talia to leave. But we are vulnerable because of her." She holds her hand against his face. "You are so naive. Not everything I have done was about saving my career. I appease the officials, the lobbyists, the diplomats, and the Coalition because it keeps me nearer to them. I know what is going on. I know their plans, and yes, in the beginning I believed in change. But I know that is no longer possible. Talia will become a target when the occupying forces arrive. She will be questioned and detained, and I pray nothing more will be done to her. I tried to stop her, for her sake, not for mine! I have not changed as much as you think I have, Alberto."

"If she was in immediate danger, why didn't you tell her, Bellona? Why didn't you tell *me*?"

"She would have loved that! Don't you know your own daughter? She would have believed her work had been effective, Alberto. Knowing that she was being watched would have thrilled her. It would have been even more motivation for this ridiculous campaign."

"Bellona, this is not just Talia's fight! You don't give her enough credit. She is neither stupid nor naive. She *knows* she is watched, that much is obvious! I have discussed this with her. She knows they follow her; she knows and she believes you sent them to watch her." He pauses. "It's what I believe too."

Alberto's candour is unnerving. His comments accurate. Things have become so complicated. "Alberto—they haven't removed me yet because they are demonstrating that Perda is still the same country. I'll disrupt their plans if they sabotage my position, that's the way it works now. Talia thinks I have done far more than I am capable of doing, good or bad. We need to think of our family now, just our family, nothing else. Talia needs to think of us for once. She needs to be somewhere she will be protected."

"Protected ... or quiet? Is this a mother speaking to me or a politician?"

Bellona squeezes Alberto's hand. He does not look at her. His wife has become a different person. Alberto needs to speak to Talia. He needs to know that she is all right. He will call her at Emil's, for Alberto is certain that Talia will have gone to her lover.

§

Talia rouses herself first. She feels a deep sadness, an aching for her family and for her life before all of this. She does not remember appreciating normalcy.

It is still early. The light outside the window from the east is a deep blue that promises dawn. Pierre will not be able to do much, but his closeness to Bellona will at least enable him to warn Talia of any trouble that she might be in. Talia trusts her instincts. Pierre seems to be a loyal friend, but Talia knows that she will be testing the limits of his friendship. His loyalties are overextended; they have been for some time. Pierre believes in Bellona's campaign. But he too is afraid of his government's recent and seemingly wilful ignorance regarding the truth behind the international economic and military interest in the region. His position is important and he is privy to important information, but his situation grows more and more suspect with each passing day for he has concealed the closeness of his friendship with Talia and Emil. Pierre's political ambitions supersede everything else in his life. His sense of duty to Bellona remains a major complication in the friendship he has maintained with Emil and with Talia since she and Emil became romantically involved. Talia is suspicious of Pierre at times, although she is moved by Emil's faith in his best friend. But Talia can't tell Emil about her greatest reason for distrusting Pierre.

Emil's heart is so good, his beliefs simple and unbending. He will convince Pierre better than she can, for he will present the issues without emotion, and with an imperative solidity.

Only when there is silence like this does the reality of what she faces find its way to the foreground of her mind. That anyone might want her to be harmed, or worse, seems surreal. But there *are* those who want her silenced, it *is* real and the apprehension that she has so carefully pushed aside emerges in moments like these, on the cusp of daylight, in Emil's arms at a time when she should feel happiest and safest. Talia sometimes thinks it would be easier just to leave Perda and to forget her involvement in this fight that she has helped to propagate. But she will never leave permanently.

It was all too easy. Her offer to head up the campaign for reform publicly was met with immediate support and enthusiasm. She told herself it was because of her education, because of her passion, her talents. But she knows these are not the most important factors. She is useful only because she is her mother's daughter. They are both being used; she and Bellona, and they will be discarded just as easily if the situation calls for it. The difference between them is that Talia is aware of this reality. Her mother refuses to see it.

The revolution must move forward. Their country, their freedom, their economy, and the people of Perda—all are being destroyed. Talia grieves the relationship she has always wanted but has never had with her mother. Any potential that might have existed for a relationship has now been permanently ruined, Talia is sure of this. Her mother has never been so disappointed in her, so angry. Bellona has changed. So many things have changed and will continue to change, for the worse. Perda will be infiltrated by foreign entities and ideologies. Its citizens will fight and be killed or devastated. Perda's economy and culture will eventually become homogenized, like those of so many other small countries in the world, in the name of internationalization. But Talia will not sit by and do nothing, say nothing. How can anyone stand by, simply witnessing the progress of greed and the makings of a false conflict? A war set in motion by people of other nations, whose military and economic ambitions have always been focused on this region. A war being manufactured by these nations, by powerful, wealthy politicians and businesses, by external forces bigger than imaginable—even by her own parents.

Emil is awake. "How long have you been awake? Did you sleep at all?" Emil pulls Talia closer to him.

"Emil, I'm worried."

"Don't worry. I'll see Pierre. He'll have heard about you and your mother—she tells him everything."

"She won't tell him about this."

"Your mother will be looking for information from Pierre."

"I don't think so. She doesn't know how close we are."

"She might know—you have to assume she at least suspects. Your mother doesn't want to hurt you, Talia, but the rest of them do. She does want to shut us down and she can, and they *will* arrest you if you give them a reason to. You have to be more wary. You can't be so casual about our safety."

"I know, I know." Talia looks at Emil firmly. "I know." She reassures him. He worries so much. "My love, I don't always trust Pierre. Be careful what you tell him."

Emil sighs. "I wish you would trust me. I know Pierre, better than you do…. We should get ready to leave."

"My father's voice last night … God."

"I know, my love, but you have to let it go. Your father has let you down too, don't you see that?"

§

Bellona watches her daughter sleeping. Talia's hands are curled into her chest, her legs pulled up to her lower abdomen. Her short hair makes her look the way she did when she was a child. The walls of the tent provide little shelter. The air is cold; it sweeps in whenever the flaps are pulled aside. The crying of the women that continued day and night in the beginning—after the takeover of the camp—has given way to an exhausted silence.

Bellona has kept to herself. She does not speak to or interact with the other women in the camp unless it is necessary. But Talia wants and needs the company of the others. She has spoken with the other women about many things. They know who she is, but they realize the importance of keeping Talia's and Bellona's identities from the soldiers, who have not yet recognized them. Besides, these other women are also from prominent military and governmental positions or families. They too wish to remain as anonymous as possible. Bellona asks Talia to refrain from acquainting herself with the others, but Talia disagrees with her mother and still does not trust her mother's motivations, even though she and Bellona have been forced together by circumstances in which they need one another.

Alberto has been dead for so many weeks. His death, Talia's life, the camp—it is all more than Bellona would have thought she could bear. But she doesn't bear it. She hasn't come to the point where she can accept that Alberto is gone, that her daughter's life and her own life are in immediate danger, or at the least, inextricably altered. She has not accepted this immense betrayal—her internment and the internment of her family—committed by the government she helped to build. *Her* government, *her* administration. A coup d'état that Bellona had not suspected would occur, not even for a moment. The soldiers will eventually know she is here, and Talia—Talia's face has been broadcast as many times as her own over the past year. It is because of Bellona that Talia is here. Bellona blames herself for all of this. If only ... Bellona needs to stay in the present, to be as protective as she can be now that the militia have taken control of the camp.

Talia and Emil speak to one another every day at the fence, and Bellona disagrees with their meetings but no longer says so to her daughter. It is important that Talia not be discovered. They have avoided recognition thus far, perhaps due only to the inadequately small force that occupies the camp. These men are militia. They are violent men, seemingly without concern for the welfare of their hostages. The men and women in the camp have learned to avoid these soldiers at all costs. To look down when a soldier approaches. To remain silent. To protest nothing. But there are half as many of these soldiers as there were of the first group. Emil has counted only three guards at one of the gates during certain times of the night. This is important.

Escape is possible.

The soldiers keep to themselves. They rarely interact with their prisoners. There is little food and almost no clean water—the only sources of hydration are contaminated wells at four spots in the camp—and people are dying, most quietly, their passings marked only by the anonymous cries and blank faces of those who are left behind grieving. This is a place of death, some dying voluntarily.

Bellona knows they will all be weakened, eventually. The only option is to attempt escape. Talia agrees.

The tent holds many women. They are all quiet. Bellona rarely looks directly at them. They do not seem to care. These women are close to broken, if they have not already given up. To what end they are being held, Bellona does not understand. She prays that Talia will never know how all of this began.

"What's wrong?" Talia whispers upon waking.

"Nothing," Bellona replies. "Go back to sleep."

§

Most of the country's citizens are still sleeping. Talia and Emil are together as they have been for weeks. They are staying at a flat owned by one of Pierre's cousins. Pierre is also with them, but he too is sleeping.

The news is trickling in, provided by the few reporters actually present in Perda, journalists that Talia admires, for they have given up their jobs, with injudicious networks, and perhaps any hope of future employment in their industry for a cause they believe in, in a country foreign to them. Talia understands this kind of passion.

The people of Perda are divided. Those opposed to the occupation have been preparing for war against foreign soldiers and their own countrymen—those who believe in the Adalardo government and the trade agreement. The coming occupation has instigated civil war. The mandate of the reform group to oppose violence and to send pleas to the participating nations has failed. Words are not stronger than weapons in this conflict, and so much of what is happening in Perda is not known because of the upheaval the media boycott has caused. The reformists initially cheered the boycott, but it has not applied as much pressure against the invading nations as the reformists had hoped it would.

Once Emil had felt a sense of hope that the power of the media was on their side. But so far, it hasn't stopped any of the plans. In the beginning, Talia too was hopeful about the boycott. Now she is discouraged that it has made little if any difference.

The Republic of Perda will soon be at war.

Even though the campaigns against the coming occupation have been going on for close to two years, she has never truly considered the possibility that her protests would ultimately be ineffectual. The reform group has transferred its remaining projects to the ACP, for the ACP shares the reformists' political agenda; however, where the reformists were not prepared for military action, the ACP is. Only Talia, Emil and a handful of others continue to telephone their contacts around the world in a final bid to halt the denigration of the Republic by the coalition of invading nations.

"What are you thinking about?" Emil leans in front of Talia and kisses her nose.

"The same thing we are always thinking about lately."

"They don't know where you are, where any of us are, not really."

"We are still prisoners here, Emil. They are everywhere. It's as though the city is already occupied. We can't leave Buena Gente, and I don't even know what is happening with my family. You should have left while you could."

"I'm your family too, Talia. You're the only family I care to have. This is my home; you are my home. This matters more to me than anything else in the world. Do you know how much you've changed my life?"

Emil's green eyes are bright and clear, his dark hair is short, and his sparse beard makes him look older, authoritative and strong. She knows he *is* strong, and unwavering in his support of her. Talia kisses him and Emil holds her tightly. She suddenly understands what he has been feeling. The worry that prompts him to plead with her to be cautious. She has become fearful for *his* life, for *his* safety. They are no longer protected by the reform group. They have led an anti-violence campaign. They are equipped for defensive responses only. Their forces are small and will be easily overwhelmed. They know this will be the case. The power they held was in their campaign for change and Talia's leadership against her mother's government. The reform cause was meant to stall or even stop the invasion. It was not built to deal with the occupation if it occurred. Talia has always been opposed to the notion that change can be brought about only through violence. But she finds herself relieved that the ACP is strong and shares the reformist mandate to keep the occupation from being successful. Talia now understands that violence is inevitable, but she hopes desperately that it will not be used unnecessarily or against civilians.

"Talia, I want us to be married. I know it isn't the time, I know marriage isn't important to you. But I want you to be my wife. I love you ... and with everything that's going on, nothing seems more important to me than us, than ... this."

"Emil, don't say things like that. Don't say desperate things. I love you and I *do* think about marriage, with you. I do want to be your wife, but don't do this now as though the sky will fall tomorrow." Talia does not intend to frustrate him. Her relationship with Emil was something she had not foreseen. He has been in her life for so many years: they attended school together as children. And then, one day, he had looked at her differently, and she felt new feelings for him within her.

At first, she was nervous and confused about her feelings for Emil. Without explanation, he had stopped spending time with her. This lasted for a few weeks. And then one day he asked her to meet him, deep in the forest near her family's property, not far from the mountains, and she asked him what she had done to offend him. He was incredulous.

Among the trees, the red, arid soil and the mesmerizing quiet he told her that she had done nothing wrong, and then she kissed him. He pushed her away. Talia was furious; she told him she knew that he wanted her to kiss him. It was this boldness, she later learned, that had made him love her.

He left her that day, but met her there the next evening, and this time, Emil told her of his feelings. He held her for a long time, and it was a night she remembered often. His love for her, like everything else about Emil, was steady.

"I want this now because I want *some* happiness to exist in all this darkness. I want to marry you, please."

Talia sees what he wants and why he is asking. "I'm sorry, my love, I make things so much harder than they need to be. Of course I want to be your wife. You make me want to be married. We will be married and it will be so beautiful. I promise."

Sirens are wailing in the distance. The ebb and flow of sound reverberates between the buildings of the city streets. The sirens are part of the new normal, part of the air-raid drills carried out many times per day.

Emil stares out the window. He is still holding Talia's hand and he pulls her to stand beside him. They look down onto sidewalks virtually empty on what used to be a city street brimming with activity. The apartment complex is one of many inspired by the art deco movement in architecture and fine art that was closely emulated in Perda during the 1950s when foreign corporations began investing in the growing metropolis. The entire urban district is like this, and as such, is one of the more fashionable spots in Buena Gente, full of restaurants, clubs, museums, *life*.

"Do you remember watching those old war movies with the air-raid sirens blaring in the background? When I was a little girl, that sound used to terrify me."

§

Sophie listens to the songs of birds. She is so hungry. Emil is still sleeping. The sky through the window looks grey and overcast. It is still early.

She rises from the floor where she and Emil have been lying against each other for warmth. She does not want to stay in this little house in the middle of the country, without any way of contacting the outside world. Sophie leaves Emil sleeping and pulls her compact from her vest pocket. She examines herself in the tiny mirror. Her face is dirty, and her hair appears coarse and heavy with dust and sweat from their trek. There is no bathroom in this small residence. Perhaps an outhouse-type building existed once, but there is no evidence of one any more. Sophie steps outside. The morning sky is filled with clouds that promise snow or rain in the mountains and shade for the rest of the region. There is a wet season in Perda, but mostly the forest is kept green by the glacial river that roves throughout the mountains, the foothills and the desert canyons. The trees and other plants are lush and coloured deep greens, despite the sandy earth into which their roots are plunged. Deep below the dry surface is a store of glacial water that constantly suckles this nation.

Sophie starts down the open pathway to a thickly treed area, where she finds a spot to relieve herself. As she lifts her jeans back to her hips, she hears the sound of machinery—the drone of an airplane, or perhaps the approach of a vehicle. She slips farther into the trees lining the pathway and runs toward the sound. As she closes in, she remains hidden, but soon can see the trucks in the distance. Three of them. Military vehicles.

Stay calm, they might just be passing through into the mountains. But Sophie does not feel calm. She knows intuitively that they are coming to the house, looking for the stolen vehicle, looking for them. She turns and, crouching, makes her way back. Once inside the house, she sees that Emil is already up.

"I hear them. Did you see anything?" he asks as he tries to peer out the door without being seen. The door is open just a crack, but he can't see anything from this angle.

"There are three military trucks. I can't tell how far away they are, maybe two or three kilometres. Where will we go, Emil?"

"I don't know. It might be a coincidence—maybe they have nothing to do with us. It might be ACP."

"And if they are looking for us …?"

"We can't let them find us. They will know who I am and who you are."

"How bad would it be for you if they found you?"

"If it is ACP, we might be all right. I am an ally. If not, if it's militia or the occupying forces, we'll be arrested, or killed. I don't really want to wait to find out. We have to go, now." Emil is watching the vehicles intently. He hopes they will pass by the farm and continue on toward the mountains. In the back of his mind, he knows that if they were simply heading to the mountains they would be using one of the many roads and not cutting their way through thick agricultural territory. He too believes this cannot be a coincidence, but hopes they are using this route simply to avoid detection and not because they are in pursuit of something, someone.

Emil leaves the doorway and walks toward the back of the house, where he opens the door and listens. Again, he looks outside. He chances a peek around the corner of the house and sees the approaching vehicles. "They're coming up. We have to get into the trees, quickly, Sophie!"

As Sophie follows him out the back door, the first spray of gunfire sounds in the distance. Then, before they have time to react, the whistle of a rocket screams in the otherwise bucolic surroundings. The explosion sends Sophie and Emil violently backward into what is left of the house, and the wooded area across from the back garden spews flames and black smoke.

§

Talia watches the other women in the overcrowded building that houses the lavatories. Their thin limbs and sallow skin are much like her own. Her body feels tired, detached, her muscles ache, and she worries, constantly. It is as though she is trapped behind thick glass and she is only able to watch life as it goes on around her. That life can exist in conditions like these seems unlikely, absurd even.

Bellona stares at the others as they move farther into the darkness of the room. The building is filthy, but warmer than the tent. Its wooden walls keep the wind out, and the women have built a small fire in one of the old woodstoves. The vent is blocked and smoke billows back into the room, but the smell is reminiscent of happier times and it masks the odour of human waste and so no one complains.

They are barely supervised. Talia believes the prisoners are not being held for any specific purpose, and this makes her father's death even more unbearable. To what end they are here, neither Talia nor her mother can guess.

"Will you speak to Emil today?" Bellona whispers to Talia.

"Yes."

"It is so dangerous, Talia."

"I know, Mother, but we're careful. We meet in a different place each day, usually where it's busiest."

"I can't believe how seldom these people speak to us. They barely feed us. No news, no explanations. It's as though we don't exist to them."

Talia laughs sarcastically. "Unless we try to escape."

"You should not say things like that where everyone can hear you." Bellona is adamant.

"They are going to kill us all. You can't believe they will let us go after this."

"I don't know what to think, Talia, except that we must remain hopeful, and that you and Emil should not be taking such chances. If they see you together, they may recognize you."

"You sound like Emil."

"Emil is as much a child as you are at times."

"Mother, Emil and Pierre are watching out for each other. You and I need to do the same. We have to take care of each other."

Bellona feels desperate. Talia is impossibly stubborn. And Emil encourages her. He has always admired Talia, followed her around even when they were children. He is doing the same thing now—and a follower cannot protect Talia the way she needs to be protected. Anger is easier than fear. Bellona chooses anger.

§

Talia feels herself being roughly shaken. She opens her eyes to the face of a woman she does not recognize.

"Wake up. I need to talk to you."

"What is this about?" Talia sits up and rubs her eyes with her open hands. She looks for her mother. Bellona is no longer in the tent.

"You are Talia Adalardo." The woman seems incensed, but she keeps her voice lowered.

"Who are you? Why are you speaking to me this way?"

The woman ignores her question. "Your mother's here too. You cut your hair, but I knew it was you."

"What is the point of this? We have not kept any of this a secret. Everyone here knows who we are. Are you threatening me?"

The woman doesn't hear Talia's questions. She has already decided what she wants to say to Talia. "You know, your own mother is ashamed of you. You and your shit army, calling yourselves revolutionaries, reformists. Look what you've done to this country—*this* is *your* fault."

Talia leans forward and whispers, "This is not the time for this. We have to help one another. I wish you would tell me who you are."

"Your name is more important than mine, Talia. Especially to *them*." The woman stands, her dark blonde hair stringy and dull, and her sharp, amber eyes fixed on Talia. She turns and walks away from Talia toward the open tent flaps.

Talia rises to her feet and manages to grab the woman by the upper arm.

The woman turns as she pulls away. "You have no idea how many lives you have ruined. You *bitch*." The woman slaps Talia's face. The others in the tent look on; some of them look stunned, some whisper to one another. One of the women is smiling maliciously, another hangs her head and shuffles from foot to foot.

Talia can't speak as her unknown accuser exits. Then she faces the others. "When did my mother leave?"

"Half an hour ago." A small voice submits this information as others in the room disapprove.

The sound of their tongues clicking leaves Talia feeling exposed and betrayed. She finds the voice in the crowd, and smiles gratefully.

§

Sophie struggles to her feet. In the smoke, she finds her way to where Emil is lying on the ground. He is dazed but alive.

"Get up, Emil, now, let's go."

She pulls him up and he stumbles alongside her. The smoke is smothering, but it is also their salvation as they run undetected through the billowing blackness into the trees behind the house. They hear another rocket pummel the wreckage of the farmhouse, but the blast is far enough away that it does nothing more in the forest than send tremors through the ground below them and smoke all around them.

"We need to get down to the river and across it." Emil is moving faster than he was at first.

"Will they follow us?"

"They'll search the house first, what's left of it anyways."

There is no time for more words. Now they are both running. Sophie periodically slows herself and glances back for their pursuers. Then she has to catch up to Emil.

The trees, the tangled mesh of vines and the lower greenery keep the soldiers obscured from view. Emil leads the way. He pushes branches aside but they whip backward, and Sophie's hands sting from protecting her face from the lashings.

They continue for close to an hour, fuelled by adrenalin and little else. Finally, the river comes into sight.

"It will be deep, and cold." Emil's voice is shaking as he runs.

"We'll try to find a shallow crossing, but we have to get across."

"Why, Emil? Why can't we just follow along on this side?"

"They knew we were there. We need to keep going, toward the border, which means crossing the river now, as fast as we can."

"That doesn't make sense." She shakes her head. "They would have come for us earlier."

"Then they must have seen you. Were you careful this morning?"

"I guess I wasn't that careful. I used the pathway to go into the trees. That's when I heard them coming. But, why attack the way they did, why not approach first?"

"Sophie, some of these people are not fighting for the sake of some greater good. They're fighting because of the instability this war has created. They're fighting for territory, for money, for God knows what. They don't care who they kill; they'll destroy anything that gets in the way. We were in the way. It's probably as simple as that."

"Good." Sophie stops running for a moment, leans over to catch her breath.

Emil slows down, watching her. "What are you doing?"

"If they don't care who we are, they won't chase us. They will probably believe we died in the explosion—that house was obliterated."

"We have to keep going."

"I am not going to swim across that river, Emil. Not if it's close to freezing. We have no food, no warm clothing, and we can't light a fire. We'll die from hypothermia before we die from anything else."

Emil leaps forward and suddenly his face is close to Sophie's. "*You* can get yourself killed. *I'm* crossing the river."

"No, Emil, we need to find a way back to the city. I know we can get help there."

"Christ, Sophie! We can't return to the city. You'll be dead before you even get to a checkpoint. We can't argue like this, you have to trust me. You don't understand what's happening here. You weren't here in the beginning of this. You don't know the groups the way I do. The ACP, the reformists, the government and the occupying forces, and the militia, God knows how many factions there are ... it's a nightmare. You have to trust me, please." Emil has taken Sophie's shoulders in his hands and he shakes her while he speaks. His exasperation is clear.

She searches his face and sees that he is sincere, committed to this course of action. She finally accepts that he is right, that fear is commanding her reason and that she has to listen to him.

"Then what? Where will we go?"

"We'll find a shallow crossing. Once we are across, we will make our way through the forest to the border. We're about twenty ... maybe thirty kilometres away."

"Thirty kilometres. Shit, Emil, they'll never let us through—"

Emil interrupts her, his hands still on her shoulders. "The border is only partially guarded. We'll get through."

THE BEAUTY OF THE WORLD

§

Talia steps outside the tent and looks around carefully. The air is cold, the sky is clear. If she looks upwards and blocks her peripheral vision, she can imagine she is anywhere but in the present. Few of the camp's inhabitants are about, the clothing they have been left in provides little warmth in the bitter air. Most of them are too weak to leave their tents. Every few days food is dropped in large buckets at the entrance of each tent. It is barely enough for subsistence, and some of it has gone bad.

Talia does not see any guards, so she makes her way briskly toward the lavatories. As she walks, she warily observes the few women around her. Emil will be waiting, and she'll go to the fence as soon as she can, but first she has to find her mother. It is important to tell Bellona about the woman that confronted her. Talia is perplexed by the woman's animosity. If for no other reason than companionship under duress, the women in the camp have developed strong bonds with one another, the kind that can only exist between people sharing amidst crisis.

Talia approaches the lavatory building from the back. As she turns the corner, which looks directly on the main barracks where the soldiers are housed, she sees the woman who confronted her approaching one of the guards. He is standing outside the barracks. His automatic weapon is slung over his shoulder and is barely visible against his green and black camouflage clothing. All of the soldiers dress this way. They all have weapons on them whenever they are on the grounds. They wear hard expressions. They don't look at the prisoners, they look through them.

Talia moves into the lavatory and calls for her mother. No response. The other women in the large, foul-smelling room follow Talia with their eyes.

"Have any of you seen my mother? She has short dark hair."

"In there." One of the women points toward a stall that was, before the water was turned off, a shower.

Talia hurries to the stall. She finds Bellona collapsed on the floor. Bending down, Talia feels for her mother's pulse, which is slow, and finds her breathing shallow. Her mother has blood on her forehead and her clothing is torn.

Talia turns back toward the other women incredulously. "Why didn't you help her? How long has she been like this?"

The women are silent.

"Goddamnit, answer me!"

The same woman speaks again. "It was the guard ... he was in there with her. He told us not to touch her after he was finished. He said he knew our faces and that he would find us."

"What do you mean after ...? He didn't ... oh my God." Talia kneels beside her mother and smooths her mother's torn clothing, strokes her face. Whispering softly, she begs for a response. She leans over and places her head against her mother's chest. *Wake up, wake up, wake up.* Her tears are fuelled by anger and grief stronger that she has ever experienced. The other women form an apologetic procession. They each glance at Talia as they pass her. Their mouths are down-turned and their eyes shifting as they move out of the room. There was nothing they could have done, Talia knows.

Bellona motions with her left hand. She doesn't open her eyes as she whispers, "I am all right, Talia, I am all right." She lifts a hand to pat her daughter's head. She can't move easily. The rape was brutal, and she is still bleeding. She doesn't feel pain any more, but she knows her body is torn. She doesn't want Talia to see any of it.

Talia lifts her head to look at her mother's face. "Mother, I'm so sorry, I'm so sorry that he hurt you. I'm so sorry, Mother, I wasn't here and he hurt you." She lowers her head against her mother's chest again.

Bellona opens her eyes and struggles to raise herself. "Stop, Talia, we can't stay here like this. I am all right."

Talia knows her mother has seen the panicked expression on her face.

"Mother, they know we are here. Tell me what to do. We have to get you some help." Talia is moving backward and trying to help her mother to sit up, when Bellona takes Talia's face sternly in her hands.

"What do you mean they know we are here?"

"A woman ... she came into the tent. She said she knew who I was, and who you were. I saw her go into the barracks a few minutes ago."

"Have you spoken with Emil?"

Talia can't stop staring. Her mother's legs are badly scraped and the beginnings of bruises colour the skin around her wrists. "No, I didn't want to take a chance until I found you. The grounds are very quiet and after the woman ..." Talia hugs her mother. She feels as though her mind might just stop, that it cannot take any more.

"Talia, you have to listen to me, you have to go to Emil. The guards will come for us. You have to tell Emil what is happening. They may have a plan. He and Pierre may be able to find us."

"But I thought you didn't want me to speak to Emil ..."

Bellona raises her hand. "Never mind—this is all we can do. Go."

"I can't leave you here, Mother. I won't leave you here like this!"

"I will go to another tent, one of the closer ones. You don't have a lot of time, Talia, go now." Bellona pushes herself unsteadily to a standing position and motions for Talia to leave ahead of her.

Talia does not have a better suggestion. She holds her mother, who was once so strong and seemingly invincible but who has been so badly damaged.

"I'll help you to the tent, then I'll go."

"There isn't time. You have to go now. I can manage, I'm all right."

Talia hesitates. "I love you, Mother. *Please* be careful. I will find you after I speak to Emil."

"I love you too—now *go*."

Talia holds Bellona and doesn't want to let go, but Bellona pushes her to leave. Talia exits reluctantly. As she steps outside, she feels as though she is crumbling into the ground like sand and that she might blow away between the blades of grass that still sway on the other side of the camp's perimeter fence. The guard at the main barracks still stands at his post, and he does not move as Talia turns toward the back of the building. She walks quickly with her eyes cast downward as she crosses the grounds. The grass inside the camp boundaries has become dry and brittle in the colder weather, and it crunches beneath her feet.

The fence is not far, and she continues undisturbed. A group of male prisoners is gathered on the other side of the fence, near an area on the women's side that is partially concealed by a small tree.

Emil is waiting, crouched close to the ground behind some of the other men.

"My love ..." Talia kneels against the fence and grips a wire triangle with each hand. She rests her forehead against the cold metal.

"I was so worried about you. What's the matter? Talia?" Emil sees that Talia is shaking. She won't look at him. Something is terribly wrong.

"The soldiers know we are here, my mother and I ..."

"What? Who recognized you? How do you know?" Emil's distress is palpable.

"Emil, wait ... they ..." Talia stops for a moment. She can't find the words. Finally, she tells him. "They raped my mother." Tears come despite her efforts to stop them. She continually wipes her cheeks with her hands and she pulls at the hair on the sides of her head. She rocks forward and back as she weeps.

Emil stares at her. He doesn't believe her, for he knows that Talia would lie to protect him. He shakes his head. He is frantic and his fingers clench the cage between them, pulling at the fence. He releases a tortured, primal sound.

"Did they touch you? Did they touch *you?*"

"Emil, stop, stop!" Talia begs him. "No ... No, *please* be calm. I am all right, my mother is hurt so badly." Talia releases a tortured whimper. "I can't think about what he did to her, not now. Listen! A woman came into our tent today—she confronted me about who I am. Then I saw her go into the barracks. We have to assume she told them we are here."

"Who was she?"

"I don't know, but she was angry. She has already told them we are here—I'm sure of it. They'll look for me."

"Where is your mother? You should not be out here like this."

"My mother told me to come, to tell you what is happening. Emil, ... it has to be now—you must talk to Pierre. We don't have a choice."

Talia glances behind and around her; no one is approaching. She sees nothing out of the ordinary. The group of men, talking in hushed voices, has moved closer to the fence, closer to them.

"Talia, listen to me. You and your mother have to hide, separately. We will find you ..." Emil knows that he is not making any sense.

A man in the group turns and shouts a warning to Emil, and Emil turns toward the sudden furore behind him.

§

Emil sees the soldier pushing through the other men. He stands to confront the soldier, but before he can gain his balance, the soldier raises his gun. Fires. The bullet glances off Emil's upper right shoulder and Emil is thrown backward.

"Emil!" Talia's voice from behind him permeates the sudden silence. The sky swirls overhead. Blood spills down Emil's arm, and the pain rips through his body as awareness engulfs him. He rolls his head to the side and watches Talia.

The soldier is no longer concerned with Emil. Instead, he points the gun at Talia on the other side of the fence. She is kneeling. Her hands are raised. Her eyes hold Emil's gaze. Her face is distorted with fear, probably for his life more than for her own. The soldier lets off a few rounds. The bullets spray grass and sand across Talia's face and body, but they do not touch her.

She continues to look at Emil, and he at her. He does not move. The idea that Talia might witness his murder is too much, so he does not attempt defiance. He must stay alive.

Another soldier, this time on the other side, approaches Talia from behind. He steps around her to confront her. He raises his pistol and hits her across the side of her face. Talia cries out. She falls to the side and her assailant kicks her in the stomach once, and then again. Talia does not move.

They would have killed her right away if they were going to. Emil's vision blurs. The soldier shouts at Talia. She does not move. She is lying on the ground, very still. The soldier kicks sand at her as he circles her. He is shouting accusations. Another man approaches. Talia is unconscious. They lift her and take her away.

Emil is left where he fell, suddenly ignored, bloodied and unimportant to them. It is Talia they wanted.

§

Emil looks toward the mountains. The river is wide in this direction and the rapids are too dangerous to chance a crossing, even though they could be shallow. Sophie waits patiently. She has reluctantly accepted Emil's suggestions and he is relieved. She is stubborn. She is also strong, but she is lost here and lost in this conflict.

The clouds have given way to the full afternoon sunlight and the cold is less intense as midday approaches. Emil walks past Sophie. They will have to move farther south to find a safe crossing. She follows. She is quiet.

"Drink as much as you can; we are both dehydrated. Don't be fooled by the cold, Sophie, the air is very dry here." Emil kneels beside the rushing water and cups his hands to drink.

Sophie does the same. The water is frigid and her hands ache after being immersed. She drinks and then wipes her hands on her jeans. "I'm sorry for being difficult. I don't mean to be."

Emil studies her as she speaks. She is a tall woman. Her eyes are dark brown, her long hair always pulled back.

"You look different than you do on television."

Without glancing up at him, Sophie shakes her head. "I look different when I'm clean too." She laughs.

He laughs also. It is good to laugh, and it is good to have company. He will tell Sophie about Talia, and about his escape from the camp, when the moment presents itself. He stands.

"Let's go."

"I'm right behind you."

The ground is loose. The terrain is difficult to negotiate, the thick bushes making their progress slow. They round a bend and the river becomes narrow, but the water still rushes. Its crisp, blue-green surface bubbles and explodes as it plummets over the rocks that protrude from the riverbed.

"We should cross here."

She shakes her head. "The water is moving too fast."

"We have to get across, and soon. This is the best place. We have to go now. We'll stay together—I won't let go of you."

"If you get swept downstream, you'd better let go." She smiles.

Emil steps into the water. "Watch your footing on the rocks— they'll be slippery."

§

Emil can't move. He is surrounded by darkness. His right arm and shoulder are numb, and he is cold. The group of prisoners dispersed when the soldier attacked him. The other prisoners left him lying there, and so he is still alone, with nothing in his mind but the image of Talia being carried away. If they had wanted her dead, they would have killed her immediately.

Emil is not the first prisoner in this camp to be injured, ignored and left on the cold ground to die. Fear of association with him will keep the others from assisting. He has to get help on his own.

"Emil." Pierre's voice emerges from the cool darkness. "I'm here. I'm sorry. I had to wait until it was dark." Pierre kneels beside Emil and covers him with a blanket.

"Pierre, I've been shot—my right ... shoulder."

"I know, I know, they told me. Just stay quiet. I'm going to bring you back to the tent. There is a doctor there. He will look at you." Pierre presses his hand carefully against Emil's wound. He stops when Emil flinches. He slowly raises Emil to a sitting position.

The pain returns as Emil is moved. "Pierre, I've lost a lot of blood."

"You'll be all right, Emil. It's not too bad. You're okay."

"Pierre, ... they have Talia."

"I know. We'll find her. Right now, I just want you to help me get you to the tent. The guards will be back around this way in half an hour, so we have to go quickly."

§

Bellona sits at her desk. She is up very early this morning. The traffic sounds outside her window will continue for another hour at least. Talia has not called, and Alberto is furious, still, even though he is calmer than he was the night before. Bellona knows he is simply frantic with worry, as she is, but for different reasons.

She picks up her telephone receiver and dials her secretary, who is regularly in the office at this hour.

"Yes, Madam?"

"Marie, is Pierre here yet?"

"No, Madam." Marie pauses. "Shall I let you know when he arrives?"

Bellona considers this. "Yes, Marie. Please do not tell anyone that I am here yet."

"Yes, Madam."

Bellona turns to the floor- to-ceiling window made with bullet- and explosion-proof glass. The window looks out onto the city of Buena Gente. The Capital Building has always amazed her, since well before she could have anticipated working in it. Its simple, grey facade is marred by the blackness of time and pollution. But somehow this gives the building more charisma, more complexity. The building's four stories are wrapped around the entire city block and at times, they contain the majority of the country's political elite. Bellona no longer feels fortunate to be among them. It is a defeatist attitude, she knows.

The people in the cars below hurry to their destinations, unaware of the betrayal they will suffer at the hands of the Adalardo government, the government they elected so many years ago. Unaware of the desolation that will be wielded against them by the occupying forces of the coalition. It will not be long before Bellona is removed from power. She has been aware of this for many weeks.

Bellona's telephone rings. She returns to her desk and lifts the receiver. "Yes, Marie?"

"Madam, Mr. Delacroix has arrived."

"Good, thank you, Marie. Wait. Where is Pierre right now?"

"He is on a call, Madam, in his office."

"Did you receive that call?"

"No, Madam. Mr. Delacroix is using his mobile."

"Fine, thank you, Marie."

Talia is with Emil, Bellona is sure of this and she is also certain that it is Talia or Emil on the phone with Pierre at this moment. Bellona sighs. She should not have asked Talia to leave their home. Bellona gathers her things and moves toward the back exit of her office. The only connection she now has to Talia is Pierre.

Bellona walks past Marie's station toward Pierre's office. Pierre's door is open and Pierre is looking through papers on his desk. Bellona enters and closes the door behind her.

§

Sophie holds Emil's hand tightly and she gasps as they wade across the river, which is churning around them. The glacial water is close to freezing, and her limbs scream with pain as she pushes them to move quickly in the icy water. The water is as high as her torso in places and the current threatens to sweep them away. Periodically, a rogue surge pounds into her and each time this happens she is sure she will be pulled downstream. But she remains upright and Emil doesn't let go of her.

As they approach the far side, the water is calmer and the depth slowly gives way to a level, sandy bed. They emerge dripping and frantic, for they need to get into the trees once again to avoid being seen, in case they have been followed. Emil resumes his lead.

The terrain on this side of the river is remarkably different. Sandy patches are interspersed with red or black soiled hills, large coniferous trees and tall, swaying grasses. On the river's banks are moss-covered stones that reveal the changing face of the region's geography. The even thicker vegetation is a windfall—it will keep them hidden.

Sophie is wet and growing colder and colder from the inside out. The dampness reaches inside her and permeates every joint, every muscle and every bit of skin that presses against her clothing. The air seems much cooler than it is. Emil is shivering too, but they push on. Emil believes it is necessary to make progress, she realizes. And moving is the only way to get warm. "How far will we go?"

"I'm not sure." Emil continues walking.

Sophie takes two steps for each of his. "Do you know this area?"

He stops and faces her, but his eyes look beyond her, darting in every direction as he watches for activity. "I've never been here before. God, your lips are blue, Sophie." Emil rubs the sides of her arms to create some friction. She is shivering uncontrollably.

"I need a minute." Sophie kneels down and looks at him. "Do you really think they'll come after us?"

"We should assume they *are* after us. I doubt that it was a coincidence that they found us back there."

"They shot everything in sight, Emil. They'll think we died in that house. Let's believe that."

"Sophie, ... I'm sorry that I brought you into this. I thought I was helping."

"I do think you saved my life, Emil—I *know* you did."

§

Pierre sits across from Emil at a small table in a café. They are seated in the very back of the narrow shop. The walls are painted a deep brownish-purple and they are covered with the framed photographs of buildings that are situated in and around the city. Alongside the photographs of the twentieth-century edifices are sepia-toned images of Perda's famous ruins. The effect of the historical contrast is dramatic. The smells are of coffee, chocolate and syrupy baked sweets, and the sounds are of percolation and chatter—bubbling and buzzing through the filled space.

It was difficult to get away from the office, but Emil had insisted. Pierre knew it was important, especially since he has not spoken with Talia or Emil in over a month.

Talia is waiting in Emil's car. Pierre had stopped briefly to say hello to her. The skin around Talia's eyes was slightly inflamed. Her mouth was softly coloured, but otherwise she didn't seem to be wearing cosmetics. She hadn't attempted to hide her fatigue or her sadness. Her long, auburn hair was pulled back haphazardly in an elastic band, but loose strands had fallen across her shoulders and in front of her small ears. She waits in the car because she and Pierre cannot be seen together.

Talia and Emil are in trouble. But that Talia has finally left her parents' home makes things more difficult for Pierre. Bellona has confronted him and he now has no choice but to act as Bellona's agent, or leave his post altogether. The latter is not an option as far as he is concerned. He has refused to see Talia or Emil since things began escalating at work.

Pierre will not tell Emil about his conversation with Bellona earlier that morning. She had entered his office unannounced, asking direct questions about his relationship with Talia. Bellona had taken him completely by surprise when she said that she asked Talia to leave home the night before. But everything Bellona suggested made sense, as it always did, and Pierre for the first time feels deeply pulled between his career and his friendship with Talia and with Emil.

Pierre's feelings for Talia complicate things further. He holds on to one memory that only he and Talia share. It happened almost a year ago. Pierre had attended a wedding with Talia at the last minute after Emil had come down with something. Pierre and Talia danced, had a wonderful time, and spoke at great length about topics—mostly politics—issues that meant a great deal to each of them. They went for a walk, and in the midst of a heated debate, Pierre turned to her. He wanted her. He had always wanted her.

He apologized immediately upon removing his lips from Talia's mouth. She chastised him and demanded an explanation for his actions. He simply explained his feelings for her and agreed never to speak of them again. Talia was promptly defensive of her love for Emil, but Pierre inferred something else from her reaction; Talia was attracted to him, Pierre was sure of it. She had readily returned his kiss. Pierre wants to believe that one day Talia will realize that she has feelings for him after all, despite her commitment to Emil.

Pierre will do almost anything to protect Talia. He knows what Bellona is capable of, and he knows what Bellona plans to do. He has almost convinced himself that Bellona's plan to keep Talia in one of the internment camps, however wrong it may seem to the uninformed or the impassioned and therefore misguided, will ultimately keep Talia safe when the war begins. Bellona is a formidable politician, a wise woman with great foresight. If she is willing to imprison her own child, Pierre believes that it is for Talia's well-being.

The ACP has threatened the government repeatedly, saying that they are ready to fight the coming occupation. The government has recently passed legislation declaring that members of the Alianza Central de Perda and the campaign for reform are traitors and that resistance to the occupation will be met with severe consequences. Pierre knows that this applies to Talia and Emil, and he doesn't want Talia harmed in any way. If temporarily removing her freedom will keep her away from the conflict, he is willing to go along with this.

Pierre believes that this occupation is good for Perda in the long term. The economic impact on the developing country will be tremendous. The provisional removal of the rights of people cannot be measured against a promising, stable, economic future, against soaring and secure prices in the global market for the region's many natural resources. The long-term effects of this occupation justify the means to this end. Emil will never understand, and Pierre doesn't try to convince him.

Pierre answers Emil's questions about Bellona. No, he hasn't seen her—he is lying, of course—and he will not speak to Bellona about Talia. Pierre has chosen the path he feels is best for all concerned, and he has remained loyal to his country and his government. Most importantly, his principles are intact.

Pierre will control one aspect of Bellona's plan to have Talia and Emil held in one of the occupation internment camps. He wants to ensure that Talia will be apprehended successfully when the time comes, for he knows how intelligent Talia is. She will anticipate something like this, she has great instincts. She will be out of harm's way in the camp, away from the war and safe from herself and the idealistic cause she has fallen into simply to spite her mother. So, Pierre insists that Talia and Emil are not safe in Emil's apartment. Emil disagrees, and at first, he refuses to accept Pierre's suggestion. But then Pierre begins to make sense, for Pierre's arguments are persuasive. Emil and Talia will relocate. They will live temporarily in a flat owned by Pierre's cousin, who is out of the country. The flat is located in a building in downtown Buena Gente, close to everything, which will make mobility for Talia and Emil much easier. Emil agrees tentatively, explaining that he must speak to Talia first. But Pierre convinces Emil to make the decision for Talia. Talia will fight the move, but she is not the best judge of circumstances surrounding her own safety. Pierre knows that this argument will satisfy Emil.

Pierre gives the address to Emil, and he gives Emil a key card for entrance into the flat. He embraces Emil before leaving the café. Pierre is doing the right thing. He has been allowed to control his friendships *and* pursue his career ambitions. He knows that he has handled this well.

§

For weeks, the local Perdan television networks have been reporting the growing presence of military personnel and equipment in the northern desert. A mass exodus of tourists and foreign nationals was captured on film by a local reporter as airplane after airplane took off from Perda's international airfield. These images were internationally broadcast, and they were enough to signify the coming conflict to those within and outside of Perda's borders.

The media boycott is helping the occupation as much as it is meant to hinder it, for the eyes of the world are not seeing the raw footage of the escalating situation in Perda provided by journalists participating in the boycott of their networks and nations. As a result of the public protest these journalists have made, their footage is in turn boycotted by all major networks. These journalists may have committed career suicide, but this does not matter to them. What matters to them is what is right and just. These journalists understand one truth, the networks are businesses, and when the raw footage is what the consumers want, this footage will become a commodity. The message will get out there, eventually, gradually.

The motivation for this occupation is simply greed—control over Perda's natural resources—as well as the many profits that come with waging war. Reconstruction is a lucrative business. The Coalition of Nations for the Occupation of Perda has their own plans for Perda, plans that the Adalardo government have not been made aware of. The Perdans must be saved from themselves—this is the public justification for war. Some Perdans agree with this notion, for they too have been convinced of their inadequacies. Even the most powerful people in Perda, including the head of the government—Bellona Adalardo—have been kept selectively informed.

The occupiers are underestimating the people of this country. The increasing strength of the ACP has been grossly miscalculated. The inherent spirit in the hearts of those whose roots go back centuries in this developing and greatly misunderstood nation will keep the invasion at bay. But the aggressors don't know this yet, and there will be much loss of life, some innocent and some not, before the first world nations responsible for this assault realize that they cannot homogenize the world as easily as they think they can. To make matters worse, evil is not carried out solely by the invaders. There are those in this region who see this conflict as an opportunity to carry out their own agendas. Wartime brings about the best and the worst in human beings. This is also true in Perda.

§

The people of Perda are unaware that this is the day designated for the invasion to begin. The sun is shining. The sky is clear, and the air is warm and sweet with the intermittent fragrance of smoke from a distant grass fire. The fires are set each summer to avoid uncontrolled wildfires, which would ravage the agricultural region in Perda. The wind carries the heady scent of the smouldering vegetation into the core of Buena Gente, where the streets are quieter than usual.

The normal bustle of the metropolis has given way to an uneasy shuffle. A curfew has been advised for the safety of residents. Most establishments have been shutting down well before the curfew. Tourists would usually provide the bulk of the patronage at the restaurants and dance halls. These businesses have not done well recently and some have closed their doors indefinitely.

Where there should be the colourful pyramids of spices, and garments designed in reds and purples and greens hanging from merchants' booths, jewellery fashioned from clay and paintings of ancient ruins, where food smells and gossip filled the air just weeks before, the market circle is almost vacant except for a few optimistic street vendors still flaunting their merchandise.

Emil and Talia are with Pierre in a tiny restaurant in the same building as the flat where Emil and Talia are staying. Pierre has been residing with them for some time now too. Bellona felt it was the best thing for Pierre to do, in order to keep an eye on Talia. And this way he can easily report back to Bellona. Pierre could not refuse; he did not want to refuse. He wanted to be nearer to Talia, even if it meant being dishonest with her. And he wants to perform his duty to his country.

Talia had protested, but when Emil asked her why she didn't want Pierre to stay with them, Talia could not answer truthfully. She told Emil she was concerned about their privacy and Pierre's proximity to Bellona. But Emil had argued that this was also a very good reason to have Pierre with them.

On this day, even Pierre is oblivious to the coming strikes. Like Bellona, he believes that the occupation will be gradual. He does not believe it will be an aggressive advance on the country. Perda is on the brink of invasion. The first attack is about to happen. Bellona will be removed from power and the government will be divided. There will no longer be any true authority in Perda.

Local police and Special Forces will attempt to maintain order, but these local law enforcement officers are stretched thinly with the numerous violent demonstrations taking place against the coming occupation. Also prepared to fight are the soldiers of the Alianza Central de Perda. They are an organized, highly trained and educated group. Their numbers are significant. Their objectives are to stop the invasion and restore peace and political stability to Perda as an independent nation. They wish to protect Perda from future invasions by moving to restructure the once progressive, but now ostensibly corrupt Adalardo government.

The campaign for reform continues its pleas to international organizations as the unofficial political arm of the Alianza Central de Perda. Talia and Emil have continued to meet with other members of the group in order to keep human rights organizations and Perda's allies informed. There has been little response from these countries thus far, for the plans for this invasion have been presented to the outside world in a very different light.

There is hope, for many have begun questioning the coalition of nations behind the invasion. The reasons given to justify the invasion are now being questioned thanks to the expanding collection of evidence to the contrary. Emil and Talia do not yet realize how much the campaign for reform has actually accomplished. There is a mounting international inquiry into the alleged justification for the occupation, but these things must be handled carefully, diplomatically—in the meantime, thousands of civilian lives will be lost in the wings of this bureaucratic process. This inquiry will eventually result in an allied force that will freeze the subjugation of Perda's peoples, but tens of thousands will have already been killed. Cities will have been wiped out, farmland will be littered with debris, schools and homes will be reduced to rubble, and the lives of many of Perda's citizens will have been brutally interrupted or ended.

There is a sound when a bomb falls. It is quiet, like a soft whistle. It is even quieter than that, more like a malevolent hissing. The whispered promise of imminent, indiscriminate destruction, assembled in a deadly parcel whirling toward the earth with a heavy head and a criss-crossed tail. This is the day it begins. The first bombers are in the air.

Talia, Emil and Pierre are drinking tea. Emil notices that Talia has been quiet for some time, since their move into the new flat.

Bellona Adalardo is sitting at her desk at home. She is questioning her decisions over the past months. Alberto is outside working on his land, worrying about his daughter, as he has been for many weeks.

The citizens of Perda are tense, but going about their lives, for they have no choice. They don't know what is about to happen.

The internment camps are established and ready to be populated. Ugly evidence of a wilfully ignorant government's naïveté. Foreign soldiers are covertly in place on the outskirts of every city.

The ACP has its headquarters in Los Vientos, a sparsely populated city in Perda's southern region. This area is isolated and the geography is unpleasant. It is an industrial region, mostly arid, and the furious winds for which this city is named are always present. Defence systems have been set up all over the country. All ACP commanding officers have checked in, their detachments ready to be deployed at a moment's notice.

Overhead an airplane drones. Unusual, since commercial flights have not been allowed in Perdan airspace for weeks.

"What is that?" At first, it is not clear where the sound is coming from. Talia holds her hand above her eyes as she looks in the direction of the noise.

"It's a plane." Pierre is gazing up to the sky. No airplane is in sight.

"There." Talia points toward the far-off ranges of the Colinas del Fuegos. "My God." She knows that it is beginning. As the words leave her lips, the air-raid sirens begin their wailing, only this time it is not a drill.

Emil and Pierre find the small plane with squinted eyes against the late afternoon sun. It is well in the distance but heading rapidly toward the city. It will soon be overhead.

"It's a bomber," says Pierre matter-of-factly, and then the realization overtakes him. "We have to go. Now!" He pulls at Talia's arm and Emil follows closely behind.

They are running. They aren't looking back, but the sleek, grey machine approaches loudly from behind and passes overhead.

Pierre stops, mesmerized. He watches the plane as it moves over the city. He begins to speak, but he is suddenly quieted as a flurry of objects falls out of the aircraft.

"Emil?" Talia shrieks his name and desperately clings to Emil's arm as the three of them stand helplessly watching the lethal objects. Despite their cataclysmic purpose, they appear to be suspended gracefully in the air.

§

Talia moves her hand slightly. The pain in her fingers is excruciating, but is not to be outdone by the spasms and the tenderness in her abdomen. She remembers the soldier kicking her repeatedly in the stomach. Her eyes are still closed. She is afraid to open them, for she does not want to see that Emil has been killed. She doesn't want to see Emil lying on the ground— shot, bleeding, perhaps dying.

Talia's face is wet and sticky. She is on the ground, but it is not the same earth that she was on when she was assaulted. This soil is fine, soft and cool to the touch of her fingers, which she then raises to her battered face. She wipes the stickiness and the dirt away from her eyes and then she opens them.

She is alone in a dark cell. The cell is surrounded by other similar cells, with the exception of one side—here, there is a gate that opens onto a corridor. A dim, orange-tinted light bulb is suspended from a cable hanging from the ceiling elsewhere in the room. The coppery smell of her own blood mixes with the damp, musty scent of the earth on which she finds herself. The cell's walls are made from the same thick wire used in the camp's perimeter fences. The space is small, perhaps only six or seven metres across, and narrow.

Talia begins to raise herself on unsteady limbs. She coughs quietly. She sits up and leans back against one of the walls. The back of her left hand is covered in gashes, and her left wrist is swollen, discoloured and stiff. But she can move all of her fingers and rotate her wrist almost normally. She feels her forehead for cuts and finds a wide abrasion that extends from the right side of her forehead into her hairline. She is most concerned about her abdomen, and so she relaxes her muscles as much as possible and presses her fingers gently into her belly. It is not distended or bloated. It only seems to be painful if she moves, and the pain seems to be muscular. She is reassured that there is not internal bleeding. She will mend, if she is allowed to. *Emil.* She doesn't know if he is alive or dead. *He was shot.* Talia is now crying softly, she slinks back to the earth, pulling her knees into her chest and holding her face against them. She thinks of him, his concern for her safety, the sound of his voice, his dark eyes, and the feel of him against her. Then she thinks of him lying on the ground, covered in blood, his face turned toward her helplessly. Emil.

Talia thinks of her mother. *Her mother.* It has been years since Talia thought of Bellona as anything but an adversary. Her mother is gravely injured, but Bellona is strong and she will find a way to take care of herself. Bellona will have heard about the attack on Talia; she will have found a safe place to hide until Emil and Pierre can get to her, and then they will come for Talia too. This will happen. It has to.

Talia believes that Emil is alive. She *feels* that he is still alive, and she knows that Pierre will help Emil. She knows that Bellona will find a way to hide. And Talia will do what she knows Emil would ask her to do. She will do anything that she has to in order to stay alive. She whispers softly, as though Emil is beside her, *I will not be careless any more.* If she had just been more careful in the first place, Emil would not have been shot.

Talia lifts herself slowly until she is standing. The ceiling of the cell is high and well above her head. She tries to stretch her arms upward but the pain in her abdominal muscles is too intense. Just as she turns to look around her, she sees a soldier walking toward her.

He begins to yell to his colleagues, who follow closely behind him. Talia moves against the back of her cell as they approach her.

"Please, *please.*" She has her hands raised as she leans toward them without meeting their stares.

One of the men opens the door to her cell. He holds his hand out. "Come now."

Talia barely understands him with his strong accent. His face is round, and he has a beard and a moustache. His hair is hidden beneath his helmet. He is dressed in military garb, greens and browns, and decorated with colourful stripes across his left breast. He is a foreign soldier. Talia nods and moves to exit the cell without taking his hand.

As she does, the soldier with the beard steps in front of her.

"Your face, it hurts?" He touches her cheek and pushes her face sideways gently in order to see the other side.

Talia is disturbed by his improbable display of concern. "I'm fine." She pulls her face away from his touch.

He lowers his hand and motions for her to walk forward.

Two of the men are in front of her and the man who offered her his hand is walking behind her as they move toward a crude concrete staircase at the end of the passageway.

The corridor stretches the length of the weakly lit room, with a wall to one side and the cells to the other. Talia assumes that she is in the basement of the main barracks. As she passes the other cells, she sees no other prisoners. *If there are no other prisoners ... they've killed them all.*

The guards lead her up the stairs. They push an overhead door open, and then they are above ground on the main floor of the barracks. She is in another corridor. The building has been constructed of wood and concrete. The beds are stacked along the sides of the wide hallway. Natural light barely squeezes through the slat-shaped windows situated every few feet just below the ceiling. Every once in a while the configuration of beds is interrupted by a recessed portion of wall in which there is a door that leads to some unknown space.

Talia keeps her head down as she walks. She feels eyes upon her. Finally, they stop her at one of the closed doors. The bearded soldier steps around her and knocks on the door. It is opened promptly, and he motions for Talia to move inside. The room is small. The bearded man steps inside with her and dismisses the other two soldiers. He closes the door behind Talia. Another man sits at a table watching her silently. There is a closed door to his left.

"Please. Sit." The bearded man places a metal chair before the desk.

Talia cautiously approaches the table. She sits in the chair as instructed. "What do you want with me?"

The bearded man sits in another metal chair perpendicular to her and to her left. He doesn't respond to her question.

The man behind the table is older, with shorn grey hair. His skin is tanned and weathered. He is now standing. He is wearing a blue uniform, not at all the same as the other soldiers. His hat rests on the wooden tabletop, tipped upward in blue with golden laurels shaped into an oval crest on the front. His blue collar, cinched with a perfectly knotted tie, is framed by his neatly buttoned long jacket. Gold buttons slide down the front and disappear behind the table. Two medals decorate each breast pocket. This man is Perdan.

"Talia Adalardo." He speaks her name as he walks behind her. He stops and leans down so that he is breathing against her neck when he speaks again. "We didn't know you were here." He laughs quietly, as though to himself, as he circles in front of her and returns to his seat at the desk.

"Bring in the woman," the Perdan officer orders the bearded man, who complies by rising and opening the door to Talia's right. The bearded man disappears into the adjoining room. Talia watches all of this silently. She is having a difficult time remaining composed. Nervous tremors cause her hands to quiver as they rest in her lap.

The bearded man returns with the woman that confronted Talia just hours earlier. The woman looks at Talia venomously. She is led forward and instructed to close the door behind her, which she does. The bearded man returns to his chair, leaving the woman standing next to the table.

"Tell us your name." The officer is speaking to the woman, but continues to look at Talia.

The woman gives her name meekly. "Liana Marcel." "Liana Marcel." The officer continues to look at Talia. "And who is this in front of me, Liana?"

"Talia Adalardo. She is a traitor," the woman hisses as she glares at Talia.

Talia stares forward, past the table. She looks out onto the camp grounds through the window at the back of the room. The window is barred vertically from the outside.

"Do you have anything else to tell us, Liana?"

"Bellona Adalardo is here also."

The officer clicks his tongue repeatedly. "Bellona Adalardo is dead." The officer pulls a revolver from a holster on his hip and fires a single shot into the woman's head. The woman falls backward; blood spraying across the wall and across Talia's face. Talia releases an involuntary cry as she throws herself back in shock. She has fallen against the chair that toppled beneath her. A woman has just been murdered in front of her.

Her mother is dead.

The bearded man is standing over her, and replaces her in the now upright chair.

If Emil is dead, her mother is dead, her father is dead, *Oh God*, she doesn't want to be saved. She wants to die like Liana and all the others. Talia is tired of fighting.

She is crying silently and staring at the woman on the floor. Blood is all around the place where the woman's face should be. The floor near the body is mottled with dark, languid pools.

The blue-jacketed officer rises and walks toward Talia. He is smiling. The revolver is still in his hand, which hangs at his side. He stands in front of Talia. She does not look up at him as he places the muzzle of the gun against her forehead. He pulls the trigger.

§

Emil protectively holds his shoulder. Even the slightest movements result in pain. Despite the pain, his injury is somewhat superficial, really. The bullet from the soldier's gun grazed the outside of his shoulder, leaving behind a large gash that has been bleeding profusely, but it will eventually heal. A doctor in one of the tents helped Emil. Pierre assisted.

After his wound is clean and Emil has rested for a few hours, Emil insists that he and Pierre act immediately. Pierre disagrees, he is concerned that Emil's injury will slow them down. Emil insists that his injury is manageable. His only concern in this moment is Talia—getting to her before she comes to further harm. The greatest danger in the plan that Pierre and Emil have calculated is re-entering the camp. The least visible point of access to the section of camp where Talia is being held can only be reached if Emil and Pierre exit the camp first. They will then have to climb an unguarded portion of the fence, directly behind the main barracks, in order to enter the camp again.

Pierre seems hesitant, but he denies feeling any uncertainty. Emil is still weak and understands that he will be a liability to Pierre during their escape, and so he doesn't ask any more questions. This is what must be done. This is what will be done, even if Emil has to carry this out by himself. His fear for Talia's life is all powerful. It shadows every cell in his body. It propels action, consumes optimism, converts faith and dispels idyllic notions. The fear he feels is the farthest thing from romantic.

"Emil, how are you feeling? Are you sure we should do this tonight?" Pierre is speaking quietly. He is seated on the cool ground in the corner of the tent, looking up at Emil, who is sitting on the cot next to him.

"It has to be tonight, Pierre. I'll go alone if I have to."

"Hang on, Emil. I'm here, aren't I? I want to go, but your shoulder ..."

"It's fine, Pierre. I feel fine. You didn't see what they did to her."

"What *about* Talia, Emil? She may be hurt. We need to consider our ability to carry her out of here, over the fence."

Emil won't listen to this. It has to be tonight. "I'm going, now." Emil lifts himself up.

Pierre shakes his head as he stands. "What kind of decision is that? You're going to get yourself killed, Emil. Maybe Talia too."

Emil pushes Pierre to the ground. "Watch what you say, Pierre. Stay here if you want to, I don't need your help."

Pierre resists the urge to point out that without his help, Emil would still be out there bleeding. Emil is emotional, which Pierre understands, but emotion makes for a reckless companion. This is his life on the line too. Pierre knows that he cannot escape alone. He and Emil need each other. Pierre lifts himself again and brushes off his jeans.

"Shit, Emil. I'm not a child. I was involved in this before you even knew it was coming." Pierre immediately regrets this admission.

Emil smugly smiles at Pierre. "And you did nothing to stop it. You did *nothing* to stop it. We're doing this now." Emil treads softly through the tent toward the opening. He doesn't care whether Pierre is following. He just wants to get to Talia.

Pierre follows Emil, despite the resentment he is feeling toward his childhood friend. They have two common goals: to find Talia, and to escape.

The grounds are quiet. Emil and Pierre can make out the silhouettes of the white canvas tents under the night sky. The camp sections are not illuminated, and so two or more sets—not much about these soldiers is predictable—of heavily armed guards patrol the tented areas throughout the hours of darkness. Emil and Pierre slip alongside their tent. Emil is only able to move as fast as he does with the help of adrenalin. The sensation in his shoulder alternates between intense pain and numbness. Emil looks back at Pierre. "Let me have it."

"They won't buy it, Emil." Pierre hands Emil a small package. Inside the cloth is a wooden object. It is merely two pieces of wood nailed together in the shape of an L, the longest portion narrow and rounded at the tip.

Emil unwraps the "gun" and stops against the canvas of a tent, four down from theirs. They are near the lavatory. "When was the last time they were by this way?"

"Over an hour ago." Pierre has been watching the guards as they walked the grounds. He has noted each time the guards move close to the lavatory, for it is located beside a large section of perimeter fence. The building obstructs this portion of the perimeter fence. This is where they will exit the camp.

Emil turns to Pierre. "Can you do this?

"I can handle it. This is the only way we can get out of here."

"I don't have the strength right now, so you have to do this. Are you sure you can?" Emil wants to impress on Pierre that it is going to be difficult.

"I can do it. I just hope that I am strong enough to do it quickly."

"You have to, before he can get his arms around you and before he can cry out."

"I know, Emil. I'm ready."

Pierre is looking away, but Emil hears something in his voice. "I'm glad you care about her, Pierre. It's good that we both want what's best for Talia."

Pierre knows that he has unintentionally revealed his feelings for Talia to Emil. He has always known that he could not hide his feelings forever. Maybe he wants Emil to know, but now isn't the time for this. Pierre is about to kill a man.

Minutes tick by, and with each passing fragment of time, Pierre is more timid about what he knows he must do. There is no other way. The situation is life or death. There is no choice and the time to act has arrived. The guards are nearing the lavatory.

"Pierre, don't think, just do it. They'll have passed us in a few minutes. You need to take hold of the first guard before that. As soon as you move, I'll be behind the other one." Emil is whispering as softly as he can manage.

"Yes. All right." Pierre can't breathe. He inhales but the air intake is minimal. The guards are very close. So close that Pierre can smell their tobacco smoke.

And then, seemingly before it begins, it is over. Just as Emil had said it would be. The first guard is dead. His neck is broken. Pierre has lifted the gun from the body. Emil has his left hand over the second guard's mouth. He has dropped the wooden "pistol" that he used to bluff. Now Pierre is holding a real firearm. Pierre is lost somewhere between disbelief and reality as he stares at the dead guard on the ground. Blinking compulsively, Pierre tries to comprehend that it was his hands that took the life from this man in less than a few seconds.

Emil removes his hand from the second guard's mouth and tells him to kneel. The guard complies silently. Emil removes the guard's scarf and uses it as a gag, which he then ties weakly into a knot at the back of the guard's head. The pain in Emil's injured shoulder has returned full force. The slightest movement causes piercing pain in his right shoulder that radiates to his hand, rendering it limp and strengthless. Emil walks around until he can see the guard's face.

"Take off your uniform, and take out your handcuffs," Emil instructs the guard. The guard is hesitant and simply stares forward. Then he lifts handcuffs from his pocket and places them on the ground. He begins to undress. He is soon shivering in the cold night air in a thin cotton, short-sleeved shirt and his undergarments. Emil kicks the discarded uniform away from the guard. "Put the handcuffs on."

The guard again complies, fastening the handcuffs onto his wrists as they hang in front of his groin. The guard is so cold, or so frightened, that he is now shuddering violently. Emil instructs the guard to kneel while facing the lavatory building. The guard lifts himself awkwardly—clumsy and teetering—and moves to the building, where he kneels once again.

"All right, undress him, hurry." Emil is pointing at the dead guard. Emil has already pulled his borrowed uniform over his

THE BEAUTY OF THE WORLD

jeans and his sweater with his good arm. He is buttoning the uniform shirt, but Pierre hasn't moved. "Pierre!" Emil hisses. "Come on, you need to hurry. I need your help."

Pierre looks at Emil. He nods. He leans down to undress the dead man, and when he is done, he pulls the dead man's uniform over his own clothing. Then he goes to Emil to assist with the buttons on Emil's thick overcoat.

They are ready. Emil takes the second guard's pistol from its holster on the uniform trousers. He walks over to the kneeling guard and hits him once on the back of the head, hard, with the butt of the gun. The guard falls over on his side, unconscious.

Pierre is the first to begin climbing the fence. The area is dark and remote. The uniforms won't help them if they are seen while climbing. The uniforms are only meant to disguise Emil and Pierre upon re-entering the camp near the barracks where Emil believes Talia is being held.

Emil musters every ounce of strength and will that he can in order to begin pulling himself up the fence behind Pierre, who is almost at the top. Emil ignores his throbbing shoulder, and the warm blood that has seeped through his makeshift bandage. Pierre is starting over the barbed wire that lines the top of all the fences. He is caught momentarily as he swings his second leg over to the other side. Because of the fleeting panic, or perhaps due to this first taste of freedom, Pierre does not descend the other side of the fence slowly. Instead, he jumps wildly and lands in the twisted thorns of brush on the exterior of the perimeter fence. Pierre is silent. Emil watches all of this helplessly. He too begins to panic. He is almost at the top, where he carefully makes his way over the barbed wire. He looks down on his friend. Pierre is shifting slightly. As Emil lowers himself down the outside of the fence, Pierre is weeping. Emil lowers himself as softly as he can into the brush. The scratch of the thorns causes minimal discomfort compared to the pain from his wound.

"Are you hurt, Pierre?"

"I just need a minute."

"We don't have a minute. We have to get away from this fence."

"Fuck, Emil. Just give me a goddamn minute." Pierre is perilously close to breaking down.

Emil is furious. Pierre's weakness will cost them their lives, and Talia's. "Pierre, you need to get it together. We're almost there."

"'I can't go back in there, Emil. We need to get out of here. We'll get help."

Emil squats in front of Pierre. "We need to get to her before they hurt her, any more than they already have. We don't have time to get help, it will be too late."

"And what if it already is too late, Emil? What is the sense in us being killed too? I won't go back in there."

"You bloody coward. You'll just let Talia die in there? You will just let her *die?*"

"Don't accuse me of being a coward! I love her too, as much as you do!" Pierre screeches and his sharp voice carries.

Before Emil can stand, they hear shouting. The other set of guards has discovered the shackled soldier near the lavatory and they are already moving toward the fence in response to Pierre's shrill exclamation.

Emil drags Pierre to his feet and they climb through the twisted branches of the brush toward the deep, desert wilderness. Emil is well ahead of Pierre when the shooting begins. Pierre is struck by one shot. He is killed instantly.

Emil can't save Pierre. Emil can't save Talia. His only choice is to continue his flight from the camp. He damns Pierre to hell for effectively committing suicide and for potentially killing Talia in the process. Emil runs faster than he ever could have under normal circumstances. By the remote knowledge and belief that Talia has found a way, like him, to survive.

§

In the early-morning purple, blue and pink welcoming of the day, Emil stumbles along through the dense juniper forest of the desert as it ascends into the Colinas del Fuegos on their northern flank. He needs to get to the city, back to Buena Gente. It is the only place he believes he will be able to find help. He would have walked for as long as necessary, grieving the death of his friend, and despite the uncertainty surrounding Talia's life. He would have walked forever if it meant saving Talia. But it turns out that he doesn't have to walk very far.

Emil has evaded recapture. His pursuers stopped searching beyond the camp's perimeter when they found Pierre. Only after querying their comrade in arms, who was briefly shackled, stripped of his uniform and found unconscious, would they have learned that there were two escapees. By then Emil had travelled in any number of directions, through the forested hills where the northern desert meets the mountains. It will be impossible for them to locate him.

He knows it is dangerous, but when he eventually makes his way to a makeshift road carved into the dry earth, he waits for passing vehicles in the shadow of a deep-orange sandstone boulder. He is not visible from the road. He listens to approaching vehicles, but there aren't any as far as he can see. He rests in this spot for close to an hour, and then he begins his pilgrimage once again. This is a remote area. Emil walks farther, into the beginnings of the alpine forest. He drags himself onward. Each step is more difficult than the last. Fatigue and dehydration have taken hold of him. He can't think clearly, or optimistically. He has never before felt such hopelessness. But then, in this one moment, his luck shifts. A rusted Jeep, the back filled with piles of wooden cases, is driven by a bald, smiling, nearly toothless, elderly man. The old man stops for Emil. Emil tells the man that his wife—for that is how he thinks of Talia—is very sick and that he needs a vehicle to get through the mountains and back to the city. The man shakes his head and tells Emil that it is too much trouble to get into the city now, and besides, he is going the other way. Emil does not plan to hurt the old man, but he needs this vehicle. He removes his pistol and points it at the driver. Emil apologizes and tells the man he isn't going to hurt him. The old man nods, exits the Jeep and motions for Emil to take the wheel. Emil shakes his head and tells the man that he will have to continue driving. He tells the man that he will release him as soon as they get to Buena Gente. Before Emil gets into the vehicle, he removes the guard's uniform that he is still wearing and tosses it piece by piece to the side of the road.

The old man watches Emil calmly, a questioning look on his face, which Emil notices but ignores. Then, at Emil's request, the old man gets back into his Jeep. Emil sits in the passenger seat. The old man proceeds to turn the vehicle around, pointing them back toward the mountains.

They drive for half the day. Emil is quiet. The old man doesn't believe that Emil wants to hurt him. He thinks that the story of the sick wife is true, maybe. The old man tells Emil about his own daughters; he has four, three of whom are living. Emil doesn't ask about the fourth daughter. He can think only of the hours passing while Talia is still in the camp.

The old man's chattering is incessant. He will tell Emil about his fourth daughter without being asked. Her name was Berta. She was just married. Well not just, it was a year ago. It was a big wedding. Many family members came home for the celebration. His fourth daughter was only married for six months when she became pregnant with his first grandchild. The old man rambles on about details, here and there. His wife was so excited. His other three daughters waited anxiously as their sister grew into a mother with each passing week. Berta lived and worked on the family farm. She was working the day the bombs fell on Perda. She ran back toward her home after the first explosions, as everyone did. The explosions were more than a kilometre from where she had been picking fruit. As she crossed the road, she was met by soldiers, home-grown militia, her own countrymen. They took advantage of her. This is what the old man says. They took advantage of her and then they cut her, in her belly, where her son was getting ready to be born. Her mother found her. Berta, the old man's fourth daughter, died violently that day, like so many others in Perda. The old man remains quiet for several minutes.

Emil is listening intently now. He tells the old man that he is so sorry. He says that he knows what this war has done to people, to families. The old man watches the road as he resumes speaking. He tells Emil that he thinks Emil is a good man in trouble. He asks Emil why he removed his uniform earlier. Emil tells him that it was a borrowed uniform, and that he is not a soldier.

The old man looks at Emil. "You are carrying a gun. You have taken me hostage and hijacked my vehicle. I think you are a soldier."

Emil doesn't try to convince this old man otherwise.

It is cool in the Jeep. The dashboard is all but stripped of its buttons and switches. Scattered across the floor, seats and dash of the Jeep are objects that seem purposeless; perhaps they are just refuse, discarded. But Emil suspects that each object is in its place intentionally, and awaiting some future purpose that only his captive is aware of.

The sky is a grey and white blanket. The sun disappeared some time ago behind this atmospheric mantle. Asphalt now streams ahead of the vehicle. On either side of the Jeep, the trunks of ancient trees with their mossy barks and vine-entwined branches linger like spirits in the woods. Emil has been watching carefully for approaching military vehicles, but they have driven past only one vehicle. It was a rundown pickup truck driven by a man physically not unlike this simple, grieving farmer. The valley that holds Buena Gente is visible in the distance as they descend into the populated region that holds the capital city of Perda.

As they draw closer to the city, Emil becomes even more unsettled. The old man tells him that there are checkpoints everywhere. But this is what Emil has to do. He has nowhere else to go. Telephone lines, electricity, water—the utilities of everyday life, normally taken for granted, are no longer accessible. Buena Gente is the only major metropolis in this small nation, and it is the only place where Emil can hope to find some kind of help.

Emil requests that the old man pull the vehicle over for a moment. The old man complies. Emil has put away the pistol. He turns sideways as far as he can toward the old man. "Please. My wife needs help. I just need to get into the city, and then I swear to you on my life that I will let you go unharmed."

The old man watches Emil respectfully and with pity. He will help his captor, because he has no choice. Despite his own terrible tragedy, he still trusts in goodness, and in the truthfulness in intuition. His intuition tells him that Emil will not hurt him. He assures Emil that the checkpoint will go smoothly. He will explain that Emil is his son-in-law. Emil agrees.

They approach the city and the first checkpoint comes into view. Emil smooths his hair, pulls the front of his sweater over the pistol and shifts nervously. As they drive up, four soldiers approach the vehicle in a lazy, intimidating saunter with machineguns slung across their chests, one hand resting on their weapons. Their camouflage uniforms are the same as those of the guards back at the camp. These are not ACP or occupying soldiers. These are militia, operating outside the conventional rules of engagement and away from the eyes of the world. The realization is a shock to Emil, who just over twenty-four hours ago watched a similarly uniformed man beat Talia mercilessly and drag her away. Less than a day ago his friend since childhood was killed by men dressed in similar fatigues while Emil desperately escaped the walls of the camp that still holds Talia in its wretched purgatory.

The old man lowers his window and waves a hand out as though greeting friends that he has not seen for some time.

Emil clears his throat as one of the soldiers approaches the driver's side of the Jeep.

"What do you want here?" The soldier leans in toward the Jeep and looks at Emil. Before the old man can answer the first question, the soldier is asking Emil who he is.

Emil takes a moment to reply, finally forcing the words from his mouth. "I'm his son-in-law. I am ... I'm helping him with his shipment."

"What's in the boxes?" The soldier is still staring directly at Emil.

The old man responds. "Just some foodstuffs, you know, some homemade things the soldiers like. We sell them. Some beer too. I have extra boxes. You want some?"

Emil keeps an eye on the soldier, who responds by spitting to the side before circling the vehicle.

The other three soldiers stand guard. Their weapons are pointed toward the earth, but their fingers are firmly rested against triggers. The speaking soldier comes back to the driver's side window. "Let me see your ID." The old man produces some papers. They are falling apart. The soldier flips through them and then he throws them into the old man's lap. "Where's the box?"

"Yes, of course." The old man exits the vehicles, goes around the back, opens the door and removes one of the boxes from the trunk. He hands it to the soldier. The soldier opens the box immediately and pulls amber bottles of cloudy liquid from their nest of straw. The old man smiles and nods, brushes the palms of his hands together and gets back into the Jeep.

The soldiers wave them through the checkpoint. They have made it into Buena Gente, but now Emil is filled with profound misapprehension. He is back in the city, and he has no where to turn, no one to contact. He doesn't know where to begin.

§

"Emil, I know we need to keep going. But I'm freezing. My hair is still wet right through." Sophie is shivering involuntarily. She is holding her arms against her chest. Her hair is so thick and long that it is still almost soaked. She is losing heat even though it has been at least four hours since they were in the river.

Emil stops. Sophie's lips are a bluish pink tone. The air isn't as cold around them any more, as the sun has reached its full height and is now starting to descend into the western horizon, but the water they were immersed in was frigid and its effects are long lasting.

"We need to do something about your hair. It'll be dark soon. You're becoming hypothermic."

Emil goes through his pockets until he finds a small utility knife. "We should cut it, Sophie."

Sophie doesn't care about her hair. She tells Emil to go ahead. He moves behind her and takes small handfuls of hair, which he crudely crops with the knife. He apologizes for pulling so roughly. Sophie holds her head forward tensely to give him leverage. She watches as Emil empties dark handfuls onto the ground.

When he has finished, Sophie's scalp aches in the places where he pulled the hardest. Her head feels lighter and she reaches up to feel the short, uneven, disordered mess.

"So how do I look?"

Emil laughs. "It could be worse." He adds, "I'm sorry if I hurt you."

"It's okay. It already feels better."

"We need to keep going. We're almost there, just a few more hours. Can you manage it?"

"I guess I'll have to." Sophie kneels and begins digging into the dry soil. She buries the cuttings of hair to hide them. "Just in case," she says as she stands, wiping the soil from her hands on the fronts of her thighs. Her clothing is already filthy. At least sweat evaporates in the arid climate instead of being absorbed by her garments.

Sophie presses her hand against a tree trunk that is thick and cool to the touch, its deep auburn bark richly engraved and sweet-scented. These trees are closely situated, and stretched between them are thick, brown, twine-like branches covered in wiry vines that have no leaves. Palm-like foliage, only on lower shrubs, obscures anything that might be at eye level. The forest floor in this place is enswathed with tiny yellow flowers that topple thin, inadequate stems.

Sophie has not truly noticed her surroundings until now. Her eyes have been constantly fixed on Emil's figure as he leads them to safety. She has not paused, even for a moment, to observe this extraordinary geography. This is the land of her childhood imagination. From a plant that looks like it is made of elongated beans composed of green rubber, hangs an impossibly magenta flower shaped like a trumpet that is drawn toward the soil by some enigmatic invitation. The flower's petals spread just enough to allow its stamina to reach through the opening.

"This country is so beautiful. My grandfather used to tell me about it all the time." Sophie leans toward the blossom and inhales with her eyes closed. The flower gives off a subdued scent in contrast with its majestic appearance.

"I have spent some of the happiest moments of my life in the forest just outside Buena Gente."

Sophie pretends not to notice the shift in Emil's voice. She won't ask questions that she knows will go unanswered. She continues to study her flower. "I'm ready when you are, Emil."

Emil is suddenly contemplating the possibility that his life has been irrevocably altered. He is imagining, perhaps sensing through some intuitive connection with her, that Talia has been taken from him. Her lifeless body uncaringly discarded, never to be touched or held by him again. Deliverance from the camp where she was discovered, beaten and taken into custody is unlikely. This abrupt, unwanted, merciless awareness settles into every aspect of his being and he no longer cares about getting to the border. He doesn't care about Sophie. He doesn't care about Perda either. The probability of Talia's extinction prompts an immediate and acute depression. A sense of dread disconnects his mind from the physical world around him and the emotional world inside him.

Sophie watches the strangeness as it is taking hold of Emil. His face has lost some of its colour. His brow is creased. His eyes are unfocused and heavy. His hands hang limply at his sides. He is simply standing there, staring as though his visual field is empty.

"Emil?" She approaches him. "Emil, please. What's wrong?"

"It's over." These are the only words that Emil can put forth. He sees Sophie standing in front of him. She looks confused, but he does not offer an explanation for his behaviour. He isn't thinking about Sophie.

"What do you mean? Emil, ... look at me, please."

"No." He walks past her.

Sophie doesn't understand. In her mind, she goes over the conversation they were just having. She tries to think of anything she might have said that would have upset him. Sophie is scared. Emil can't lose it, not when they are so close to the border. She can't do this on her own. This isn't only about her, either. She wants to help Emil. She wants to believe that there is hope for Talia. She places her hand on his back.

"Emil, everything is going to be okay. Tell me what you're thinking about."

The sensation of a woman's hand pressed against him, the concern in her voice. Emil responds with anger and hostility, not toward Sophie, but instead toward an absent, speculative enemy that he cannot see or defeat in time to save Talia. Emil crouches, he is shaking, his hands are fisted as they tear away at an invisible barrier before him, and he stumbles forward and falls on his knees.

Sophie stays back. Emil is weeping, his head forward, his chin against his chest and his arms hanging to the earth. He is defeated and broken and Sophie can't find the words to disentangle him from this despair.

"I want to help, Emil, tell me what I can do."

He slips further into his grief. Sophie sits beside him and waits for him to say something.

Emil sits back after several minutes. He doesn't look up. He is calmer. "Sophie. What if she's gone?"

He wants to tell Sophie everything. He wants to tell her about Talia, and so he does.

§

They don't wait for the bombs to meet the earth. Emil leads the way into a small clothing store, shouting to the people inside that the city is being bombed. There are just four or five others inside the store and they are running toward the windows, gasping.

"Do you have a basement? You ... there ... do you have a basement?" Pierre is screaming at a young man behind the counter, who is staring out the window and up toward the sky.

"Forget it, Pierre." Emil leads them into a backroom where he finds a door that leads to some stairs.

They have only descended the stairs halfway when the bombs land and detonate just inside the western end of the capital city of Perda. Everything happens in a blurred moment somewhere between possible and impossible. These are conventional bombs, non-nuclear. Radioactivity is not an issue. But the shock waves are devastating nonetheless.

Some of the buildings near ground zero are completely levelled. More aircraft approach and they too release their deadly cargo. More explosions rip through the city and its surrounding area. Downtown, the buildings in Buena Gente are partially destroyed. Debris flies through the air—lethal projectiles of glass from shattered windows, metals and plastics from twisted vehicles, and pieces of human bodies—and after the initial blasts, thick, dark clouds of concrete dust and smoke fill the air and block out the daylight as buildings begin to collapse. Everything is on fire as electrical lines inside buildings and outside in the streets are severed, their exposed wires sending sparks into various inflammable materials. Smaller explosions are set off when gases from damaged natural gas pipes meet with sparks from the live electrical lines.

Talia pushes pieces of plaster and wood away. She crawls to Emil. His face is covered in a chalky residue. He seems to be unharmed. He asks her if she is all right; he inspects her face and sees that she has just minor cuts and abrasions. Pierre has already gotten up and is investigating ways out of the collapsed stairway.

When the bombs detonated, Pierre, Emil and Talia were thrown down the steps into what appears to be a cold storage room. The walls around them have been reduced to litter. Dust clings to every part of their clothing and skin. They pull their shirts up over their mouths to keep from breathing in the fumes.

"The stairs are covered. We have to climb out. Emil, hold on to my sweater. Talia hold on to Emil." Pierre waits for Emil to tug on the bottom of the sweater. Pierre leads the way slowly and carefully, climbing upward toward the bit of light that is still visible. He warns Talia and Emil of broken glass, jagged bits of concrete and splintered wood as they crawl to the surface. Finally, they emerge from the rubble into shrouded daylight. They are coughing. The air quality is almost as poor on the main level. Emil calls out to the others. There is no response. The shop is almost destroyed. Fires are burning in buildings across the street. Spontaneous blasts echo throughout the chaotic scene that just minutes earlier was a calm afternoon in the city.

"My God." Talia has found the young man from behind the counter. He is burned badly and breathing shallowly. His hair has been singed from his scalp. His skin is blistered and raw, and his clothing burned into his skin and covered in soot. He is unconscious. Talia kneels on the floor and holds his head in her lap. She pants as she notices the body next to the man. It is barely distinguishable as a human form. She closes her eyes when Emil kneels beside her.

"He'll die Talia. You can't do anything for him."

She looks up at Emil. "I can hold him at least."

Emil sighs. The expression on Talia's face—of such profound empathy and childish hopefulness—breaks his heart. He walks forward. There are huge holes in the storefront where the windows and door were. The street is deserted; mangled vehicles are displaced onto sidewalks or in the middle of the road. The air-raid sirens continue to sound, as though their persistent cries can somehow buffer the city from further destruction.

"We've got to leave. We have to get to my office." Pierre stands beside Emil, speaking quietly.

"What the hell are you talking about? We can't just leave these people." Talia is crying. Her body trembles. The young man in her arms makes a strange sound, a loud gurgling, and then he is quiet. Talia begins to sob as she holds him.

"Talia, we aren't safe here. We need to get to the office. I will talk to the people I know. They'll help us."

"They'll *help us*? This is what they wanted, what you wanted, what my goddamn mother wanted!" Talia screams at Pierre. "How can you think *they* will help us?"

Pierre remains calm.

"Talia, my love, calm down. He's just trying to help." Emil knows that Talia is headstrong and that she won't easily back down when an idea has rooted itself in her mind.

"It's okay, Emil. Talia will believe whatever she wants to believe." Pierre's sarcasm is aimed at Talia as he looks pointedly at her. "Let's go to the Capital Building. If for no other reason than that we'll be safe there. Maybe we can hide."

"Pierre, really. Do you think we'll get anywhere near the building?" Talia has gently placed the dead man on the ground. After every few breaths that she takes, she is forced to cough. "Emil, why aren't you saying anything about this?"

"My love, I'm sorry, but I think that Pierre is right. We will be safe there, at least."

"How do you expect us to get there, Pierre? And what if my mother is there? My father, Emil. My father. I have to know if he is safe." Talia is begging Emil to listen to her.

"We'll know more when we get there. We should leave now." Pierre has softened his demeanour.

"Where is everyone? They're all dead. They're all dead. Emil." Talia is crying and clinging to Emil. He holds her against him as they leave the shop. The air has begun to clear and sunlight drips into the aftermath of the explosions.

Emil consoles her. "I know, my love. We're going to find help."

"You can't believe that I knew anything about this. I swear to you on my life that I didn't. I would never ..." Pierre's voice is rough, more with emotion than because of the dust and smoke. He too is questioning his government, mostly Bellona. He didn't anticipate these attacks. This is not what was supposed to happen.

"Whatever you say, Pierre," Talia offers quietly.

Haze and smoke are suffocating the buildings of this downtown neighbourhood. The three of them walk closely together. The buildings that border the street are remarkably intact. Most are still standing, though missing many of their windows. The smaller, stand-alone buildings took the brunt of the blasts. Their skeletons are exposed and their viscera are indiscriminately scattered.

People are beginning to emerge from their hiding places. Those still living are blackened, scraped and bloodied. They collectively display an expression of stunned desolation.

Vehicles have started moving again in the streets. Their drivers steer them recklessly around obstacles. Terror has found a home in the good people of Buena Gente.

Pierre begins trying the doors of parked vehicles. Finally, he lifts his foot and with the heel of his boot, he kicks and smashes the driver's window of a car. He reaches in and unlocks the door. The driver's seat is covered in glass fragments, which Pierre carefully removes. He sits in the car and reaches across to unlock the passenger doors.

"Get in, let's go." Pierre is reaching under the steering wheel and pulling out wires. He has closed his door.

"Emil, I don't think we should go with him." Talia holds Emil's arm, keeping him from getting into the car.

"We can't stay here."

"I know, but maybe we should go to my parents' house. They have the shelter."

"No. It's too far; we won't make it out of the city."

"Then let's find a safe place to hide," she begs. "Listen to me, my love. They might ask us questions, and even hold us for a little while. But at least we'll be safe at the Capital Building."

"Safe?" Talia raises her voice slightly. The car is choking and sputtering as Pierre attempts to get it started. "Emil, come on. We're traitors according to them. The last thing that we are in that place is safe. We've spent the last few weeks hiding from them, and it was Pierre's *suggestion* that we hide. Why would he suddenly *want* us to go there?"

Emil shakes his head as he scrapes his boot forward and backward against the sidewalk. He is thinking. He looks at her, he shakes his head again. The car has started and Pierre is motioning for them to get in. Emil glances about and then tells Talia to wait a moment. Emil opens the car door and he sits inside. He closes the door.

Talia waits on the sidewalk. She spins slowly, looking upward and around her. She watches the sky expectantly. She watches Pierre as Emil is speaking to him. Pierre is laughing, but Talia can see that it is sarcasm and disdain that fuels his laughter, and not good humour. Emil finally gets out of the car.

Talia waits for an explanation as Pierre suddenly jerks the car forward and disappears around the corner.

"What did you tell him?"

"I told him that we felt it was safer for him to go alone. I said we would wait for him in the flat."

"But how can we?"

"They won't strike this area again. We'll be safe here for a day or two. We'll go back to the flat. If Pierre doesn't return, we'll decide at that point what to do."

§

Despite Emil's insistence that she move away from the windows, Talia has to watch everything that is happening outside, to their city, to their country. The apartment building is all but deserted. They are among a handful of people who have taken refuge in the otherwise empty complex. She has tried to contact her parents, but every phone line is down, mobile phone service has been interrupted and everything in this new world is chaotic, and dark. There is no electricity across the city. The opaque blackness of the area in the moonless night slithers below the windows with malicious intent, broken up periodically by the distant exchanges of ammunition.

The sirens have been screaming their futile alarms on and off from the time the first bombs were dropped. That was earlier in the day. Emil and Talia have been waiting in the flat for Pierre to return, since there is no way for him to contact them otherwise at this point. Since the first strike on the city, additional strikes have been carried out in the distance, and now a full-scale battle is underway. Talia has been watching it all incessantly. She doesn't even look away when she speaks to Emil. Orange flares and the bright white of anti-aircraft rockets streak across the deepest blue of the night sky. Evidence of death and destruction is not as apparent as it was during daylight hours. There is nothing to see now, but for a show of lights accompanied by the dull, muffled sounds of far-off explosions. Mortar attacks blaze across the sky like fireworks, and Talia can almost fool herself that this is a celebration.

She has thought about nothing but this occupation, *invasion*, for over a year and yet she was thoroughly unprepared for it, she realizes this now. Perda is at war. *Perda is at war.* This doesn't make sense, it isn't real. It can't be. Distant thuds indicate shells hitting their targets, or some target somewhere.

Emil is worried because Pierre has not returned. Emil and Talia cannot stay in the flat for very long, for the building is probably damaged and possibly unsafe, and eventually this area will be hit again, sooner rather than later since Buena Gente is the capital. Then again, maybe the occupying forces already would have levelled the city if they were going to. The capital city of Perda accommodates all of Perda's governmental offices. Perhaps those have been occupied and the occupying forces will not chance the accidental destruction of useful edifices. The occupying forces would, therefore, leave the city relatively unscathed.

Emil's guesses are based on very little information. He did not anticipate a day like this. Never did he imagine that the occupation would begin this way. It was going to be gradual, selective; brute force was to be used only if violent resistance was encountered. And now Buena Gente is in chaos. Its people injured, scattered and terrified. Unidentifiable bodies still lie in the streets, or they are buried beneath the rubble of fallen structures, unclaimed.

The claustrophobic atmosphere of the small flat in the crumpled building in the air laden with the odour of smoke and the reverberation of acts of war is becoming more and more repressive. But Emil doesn't know where they will go if they have to leave this place. Emil's apartment is even closer to the hard-hit industrial area, and it is surely damaged if not destroyed. Both Emil and Talia have been affected by the bombing, but Talia seems profoundly disturbed since the raid on Buena Gente. Emil doesn't try to convince her to move away from the window. She won't abide by his advice in any case. She doesn't look away from the fiery spectacle of combat.

Emil can't just sit here uselessly. He has already collected containers of juice and water as well as nonperishable food items and placed them in a bag. All electrical devices are useless, unless they have batteries. *Batteries.*

Emil lifts himself and runs in the dark to the bedroom that he and Talia have been sharing. Along the way he crashes into furniture and curses. He chides himself for being stupid as he raises the alarm clock radio that is plugged in and therefore seemingly of no use. He turns it over and feels its underside— sure enough; it has an empty slot for two batteries. Emil unplugs the radio and takes it with him. He begins rooting through drawers, checking for batteries with the tips of his fingers. In the hallway there is a table, and above it, three shelves connected to the wall. On the shelves are boxes and magazines and books. In one of these boxes Emil finds a flashlight; he tries to use it but it too is without a power source. He pulls things out of the box until his fingers feel the slim, cool cylinders of batteries. The batteries are too small for the radio, but they fit into the flashlight. Emil turns it on and begins rooting through the remaining contents of the box. He realizes that he has discarded an unopened package of batteries on the floor. He opens them and finds they fit into the radio.

"What are you doing?" Talia has been distracted by his rustling, and now she is beside him.

Emil points the flashlight toward her. Talia squints and lifts a hand to the light. "A radio and a flashlight. I found some batteries."

"Will we be able to pick up a signal, with all of this going on?"

"We'll see in a moment. How are you, my love?" Emil doesn't look up at her as he asks this question; instead he is focused on getting the batteries into the radio.

"I'm fine," Talia responds. Her voice is devoid of inflection. She walks back toward the window. "You should bring it closer to the window. We'll open the window. Maybe that will help." As she suggests this she is already doing so.

Emil carries the radio to her. He is holding the flashlight in his fingers and shining its beam forward so that he can see where he is going. As he does this he has turned the radio on and he is moving the tuner slowly through the various frequencies. The crackling and hissing of empty airwave static fills the room. Emil keeps the volume turned up high to avoid missing tentative stations that may not be readily audible. As he moves the tuner slowly forward and backward, the quality of the interference is unchanged. Emil is disheartened. He switches bands and suddenly a female voice is broadcasting. Talia turns away from the window and settles next to Emil.

"... attacks have been underway for several hours in the northern and central regions of the country."

A man's voice interjects. "Sophie, we understand that all foreign journalists in the region have been warned to stay indoors and out of the streets of Buena Gente. Are there many foreign journalists in the region?"

"Well, Carmon, there certainly are not many of us here. Without the support or protection that is usually afforded to journalists in combat zones, we are counting on one another now that the invasion has taken place."

"We keep hearing the word invasion. This *was* supposed to have been a gradual occupation, was it not?"

"Yes, as has been reported, at least until today, the Adalardo government was in support of this occupation. Bellona Adalardo set a historic precedent in this area of the world by sponsoring the foreign occupation of this nation in order to force the stabilization of the economy surrounding Perda's natural resources. All of this has prompted violent protests. These protests have been taking place throughout Perda, and across the globe, for months now."

"Sophie, what has happened to the Adalardo government over the course of the day? Have any statements been issued?"

"There is absolutely no news as of yet. These local reports, like the one we are doing right now, are really the only source of information out there at the moment. We are trying to get video footage together to send it out to international agencies, but the media boycott has successfully impeded our ability to get this footage delivered to the few networks around the world not participating in the boycott. News is trickling out, but so far nothing has been said about Bellona Adalardo or her government."

"We'll just remind our listeners that we are speaking with Sophie Panos in Buena Gente, Perda, where the occupying forces of the Coalition of Nation for the Occupation of Perda have taken over the capital city of our neighbouring country earlier today in what was supposed to have been a gradual occupation, but which has turned into a full-scale invasion. Sophie, please describe the scene in Perda tonight."

"Right now the capital city is without electricity. Apparently, generators are being used wherever possible, but the city of Buena Gente seems to be completely blacked out. I'm not sure how much of that is due to the power outage, and how much of that has been voluntary from the time that the air strikes took place this afternoon. We are still seeing and hearing explosions and anti-aircraft fire, but these attacks seem to be largely in the northern and southern regions of the country. There have not been any further strikes on Buena Gente."

"Sophie, can you tell us more about the media boycott? Why such a strong reaction to the occupation if it was not previously known that it would be carried out as an invasion?"

"The occupation was never supported by the United Nations. So, regardless of the rhetoric used to describe the plans for this occupation, or invasion, the move was well outside of being sanctioned."

"Sophie, as a journalist myself, I find it difficult to understand how avoiding coverage of this war will punish the perpetrators of the invasion."

"I agree, Carmon. Although, 'boycott' is really a misnomer here. Journalists *are* covering the event, but they are refusing to do so under the umbrella of their networks, at least those who were working for networks with interests in seeing this occupation carried out."

"So, what you're saying is that journalists reporting in Perda are doing so of their own volition?"

"I guess you could say that, Carmon. The nations taking part in this occupation have slapped regulations on what is being shown on the news domestically. They have violated the democratic right to freedom of expression, and they have placed immense pressure on media networks. I would say that the majority of journalists participating in the boycott are former employees of these networks in question and citizens of the nations in question."

"What do you believe this boycott will accomplish?"

"Occupations like this by wealthy, globally influential nations operating outside of UN counsel have been allowed to take place elsewhere in the world over the past five years. This has set an incredibly dangerous precedent. Journalists participating in the boycott claim that despite efforts not to do so, they inadvertently contributed to these operations by providing coverage to networks heavily sponsored by companies with interests in the affected regions. It is this conflict of interest that has decided this course of action in the media industry."

"So what kind of message does this send out Sophie?"

"The United Nations is an essential organization, albeit bureaucratic. When nations begin mounting operations that blatantly go against UN recommendations and regulations, well, we are seeing today what can happen. The boycott puts pressure on pocketbooks. Many journalists have chosen not to participate one way or the other. There have been threats against journalists by representatives of the Coalition of Nations not to provide freelance coverage of the invasion. Many of my colleagues are, quite rationally, afraid of ruining their careers."

"Why are *you* here, Sophie?"

"I've chosen to be here for personal reasons."

"Can you share those personal reasons with us?"

"My grandparents were born in Perda. They lived here until I was thirteen. I wanted to be in Perda for this, to witness the occupation and to document the occupation."

"Sophie, thank you so much for speaking with us. Please stand by and we'll speak to you again soon."

"We've been speaking with Sophie Panos from Buena Gente. We must point out that Sophie is not one of our usual correspondents, but like many of her colleagues stationed in Perda. Sophie kindly agreed to speak with us as our own correspondents have not been permitted in Perda for the past two months. Many of you have seen Sophie's recent television reports on the coming occupation. There are many issues surrounding this occupation, not the least of which is the refusal of the coalition of nations responsible for this invasion to categorize it as such. So far all explanations given suggest that this is a strategic military response to the alleged growing instability in Perda. The Adalardo government has not issued any statements thus far. However, the Coalition of Nation for the Occupation of Perda insists that the objectives of this occupation are two-fold—the securing of this territory before enemy forces can take hold of it and the liberation of Perdans from further economic or political instability. Our neighbours in Perda are no doubt listening to this broadcast, so we'd like them to know we are here, we are watching and we are doing our very best to get this news out to the international community. I am Carmon Vasquez—we will be back on the air in a short moment."

"My God, Emil. What is happening? Where is my mother? And my father? Oh my God."

Talia's reasserts her defining rationality.

"I can't believe they are even allowing theses broadcasts."

Emil hates seeing her this way. Fighting her emotions, she is digging in and refusing to allow herself even the slightest display of sentiment. "I'm sure they are safe, my love. Your mother must have known this was going to happen. She must have known."

"What if she *did* know, Emil? My God. She did this, to all of us."

§

Emil is in the small kitchen of the flat. He is putting together something to eat. Talia continues surveying the chaotic beginnings of war from her window perch. Emil is considering their next step. They cannot stay in the flat, for the bombers might return to finish off the city. Nowhere in Buena Gente, or Perda for that matter, is safe at the moment, and leaving the city might be a dangerous decision.

And then there is a gentle knock. *Pierre.*

Emil is the first to the door. Pierre is standing in the hallway. He is alone. Emil embraces Pierre before letting him into the flat. Talia is waiting inside. She asks Pierre why he has taken such a long time to return.

"Things are very bad … it's fucking awful out there. It took some time to speak to the right people. We need to hurry. Are you both all right?" Pierre moves without hesitation into the flat. He immediately begins gathering things. "Put together a few things, clothes, identification. We are going to stay at the Capital Building."

"But what about the occupying forces? We'll be prisoners." Talia refuses to go to the Capital Building. She doesn't believe that Pierre is even suggesting this course of action.

"No, I explained the situation. It won't be like that. They want to help. We'll be safe."

"Yes, *you'll* be safe. What about us, Pierre?"

"I don't know, Talia. I can't tell you anything else. You should come with me. What other choice is there right now?"

"What about my parents?"

"I don't know anything about them."

"Come on. You don't know anything about my mother?"

"Talia, I don't know what your problem is with me right now, and I don't care what you believe. That's the truth."

Emil steps in and tries to get Talia to relax, but she resists his attempt at peacekeeping. She is persistent. "Emil, we can't go. I'm telling you. We are safer on our own."

"My love, I don't know what else to do. At least we'll be safe … Pierre, can you give us a minute, please?"

"Sure." Pierre walks into one of the bedrooms.

"What is going on with you and Pierre? Why are you being this way with him?"

Talia can't tell him about the kiss, about the guilt she has felt ever since. She can't tell Emil that it is possible that Pierre is thinking with his heart and not his mind. She can't tell Emil that she doesn't trust Pierre to do the right thing any more. She knows Pierre is a good man, but his position in her mother's government means that he cannot be fully trusted, ever, no matter how strong their friendship is.

Talia hates to lie to Emil, but says, "It isn't Pierre. I don't trust anyone any more, except for you, my love."

Pierre hates being excluded while Talia confides in Emil. He storms back into the room impatiently. He's had enough. "Talia, for God's sake. They want to help us. What else can you do? You can't get out of the city. They've bombed the whole fucking country. You are an Adalardo. You're valuable to them, they won't hurt you!" Pierre wants to shake her. He wants to hold her in the same moment. He wants to tell her how much danger she is in, but he can't do so without implicating himself. All he can do is try to protect her. At least in the camp she will be safe, for Pierre knows about the internment camps and he knows that Bellona has made arrangements for Talia and Emil to be taken into custody, for their own protection. Pierre will see them to the camp, but he won't ever let them know that he agreed to this. He tells himself repeatedly that this is the right thing to do, and that it is the only way to guarantee Talia's safety.

Talia flies at Pierre. "Exactly! Don't you see that they will use me? They have ousted my mother. What makes you think I am safe? Forget it, Pierre. I'm not going!"

Pierre runs his hand over his head in exasperation. He sighs and stares at his feet. He knows Talia too well. She won't budge, nor will Emil because he trusts Talia's judgement about these kinds of things. Pierre waits a moment before speaking again calmly. "Talia, at least let us take you to a safer location, closer to the Capital Building. The area is secure. You can't stay in this building. They'll hit this area again. There's fighting in the streets. The militia is strong and they are moving across the city quickly. Please."

Emil looks at Talia. "We should go with him. Just closer to the Capital Building. Just to be safe. We'll find a place to wait there until we decide what to do."

Talia shakes her head as she contemplates this plan of action. She feels trapped. She watches Pierre's face. She knows that he cares about her. She knows that her questions are becoming tedious. Finally she agrees despite her reservations, because she cannot think of a better solution.

Pierre is relieved. "Good. Pack some things; they are waiting for us downstairs."

"They? You didn't come alone?"

Pierre's frustration is evident. "I was escorted. How else could I have made it back here?"

"Okay." Talia won't push any more. Emil clearly wants to go, and she believes in Emil.

Talia and Emil throw some food, clothes and toiletries into a bag. Pierre puts together a bag of his own things. He'll need them while he stays at the hotel near the Capital Building with the other governmental officials. He has not been allowed to see Bellona yet, but he expected this. He imagines that she is busy, debriefing the leaders of the occupation.

Talia, Emil and Pierre are asked to sit in the back of the waiting vehicle. It is a military van. An armed guard sits with them. They are told that this is simply a precaution. The doors are closed behind them. They will be in this vehicle for hours. They are as yet unaware that they are being transported to Camp 1— one of three internment camps situated in remote locations across Perda's desert region, established by Bellona Adalardo and the Coalition of Nations for the Occupation of Perda. Pierre knows this, but he does not know yet that he too is on the list. It is not long after they depart that Talia begins to hurtle demands for information. Emil becomes uncharacteristically demanding when Pierre is deflective, and then Emil becomes enraged. But their questions are ignored, and then silenced by the muzzle of the guard's gun as it is pointed toward them.

They are formally ordered to silence themselves. They are told that they will have answers soon.

Talia looks at Pierre accusingly; she charges him with betraying them. Pierre responds angrily that he is also being held and that he is tired of Talia's accusations and paranoia. Emil becomes calm again. He implores Talia to do the same. He asks Pierre outright if Pierre knows anything about what is happening. Pierre swears that he is just as concerned and staggered by their sudden captivity. Pierre demands answers from the guard and he too is warned.

It is only after they have reached the camp that Pierre realizes he too is to be interned. His ideas, his principles and his politics have been useless. He realizes how insignificant, misguided and malleable he has been in all of this.

Talia is inconsolable. Her anger has turned to sorrow. After going through the intake process, after they have been assigned clothing, bedding and a tent number, after they have made their way to their tent—the hesitant footsteps of the newly imprisoned—she sees her father in this place, standing in the door of the tent that she and Emil have been assigned to. She runs to him.

Alberto has not seen or heard from his daughter in weeks. He will not speak of the disgrace Bellona has brought to their family. He will not tell Talia that her own mother planned this all along, only to have it backfire. He simply wants to hold Talia, to let her know that never again will he allow anyone to come between them.

Bellona stands next to Alberto, expressionless when she sees Talia for the first time since Talia's expulsion from their home.

Alberto has not spoken to Bellona, nor will he look at her, since they were brought to this place. Culpability leaches from her with every breath. Talia won't look at her mother as she holds her father with childlike intensity. After their greeting, Talia listens to her father explaining that they are all being held indefinitely by the occupying forces, that the conditions are good and that at least they are safe. Talia doesn't say to her father that because of her mother's government, no one in Perda is safe any more. She has noticed her father's demeanour toward Bellona, and she suspects that he already comprehends everything too well.

Pierre is stunned when he sees Bellona standing inside the tent. Everything is wrong. They have all been used. They have all been lied to. And some of them have done more lying than others.

§

Emil is keeping to himself. Perhaps he is embarrassed about his display of emotion, perhaps he is exhausted with worry, or perhaps—more than likely, in fact—he is thinking of Talia.

Sophie can only imagine what he is going through. She can't help but feel that Talia must be dead at this point, but she does not say this to Emil. She doesn't want to dash whatever hope remains for him. Emil has not spoken since his revelations about Talia and the things that he and Talia endured after the camp was overrun. Sophie cannot believe that Bellona Adalardo was interned, along with most of her government. All of these things transpired covertly, without intervention, without consequence thus far for the perpetrators of these war crimes, including former members of the Adalardo government. Sophie almost finds it hard to believe, and were it not for Emil's distressed recounting of the recent events of his life, she might not have believed him. No one else will believe the things that he spoke of. No one will believe that Bellona Adalardo was held captive, and then raped in an internment camp of her own design. No one will believe that Talia Adalardo found herself in the same internment camp, with her mother, despite their polarized political careers. Nothing about this war against the people of Perda, because that is what it has become, is valiant or representative of the intent to liberate. This is a hermetic war fuelled by greed and dishonesty.

Sophie thinks all of this as she marches, now ahead of Emil, in the late, late afternoon light. It will soon be dark. The trees have given way to less dense vegetation and meadows filled with low, rubbery shrubs that jet out of the sandy red earth like cacti. Perhaps they are cacti, or the cousins thereof. Bluish juniper bushes stretch out as though yawning, their prickly, bristled evergreen extremities knotty, twisted and beckoning.

Sophie is carefully placing each step for fear of treading on some unsuspecting, venomous creature. She stops for a moment to look around her, waits for Emil to catch up. "How are you doing, Emil?"

"I'm okay—better, I think."

"Good." Sophie is relieved, because she needs Emil in order to find her way out of this, and because she has grown to appreciate his company. She wants to help him too.

"We're near the villages," Emil offers as he stares into the distance. He is referring to a strip of land just before the border, which is inhabited by ethnic villagers. "We need to be careful. Let me do the talking if anyone approaches us."

"What if they recognize me?"

"Sophie, these people don't have televisions."

Sophie immediately feels foolish. "Right."

"We should be just a few kilometres from the border."

"Okay. Lead the way, then." The border could be guarded. In a few hours she may be captured, or killed. Sophie is once again afraid, but also anxious to keep moving, to keep doing … something, anything.

Emil moves steadily and briskly forward. Admitting to himself that Talia may have been killed is the hardest thing he has ever experienced. But he has regained his composure, and a semblance of hope. He has to hold on to the possibility that

Talia is alive, no matter how impossible it seems. He won't give up on her, not until he sees for himself that she is gone. Sophie had listened quietly and murmured only words of encouragement, without the promise of false hope. She did not offer sympathy, just an ear, and that was all he had needed in order to open up.

As they move through a clearing, they round a sandstone butte that sits like a fat, melted female figure in the sand. These sandstone formations are everywhere in the distance. Near them are piles of boulders coloured by the reds, greys and yellows—indicators of volcanic geography—of iron, sulphur and carbon that mar their surfaces.

On the other side of one of these piles, Sophie suddenly hears chatter coming from far away. Emil hears it too and he pulls her aside, behind a pile of stones. He leans around the barrier to watch the people in the distance.

"Is it safe?" she asks.

"I don't know. These villages are so isolated."

Emil focuses on the would-be buildings that make up the village. Some of the buildings have collapsed, or burned. The ground beneath them is scorched. "This village was hit."

"Hit?"

"Bombs, or rockets, who knows."

"But why? What kind of threat do these people present?"

"I don't know. Let's go. Remember, please, let me do the talking."

"Emil, what if they are armed? What if they are afraid of us? Will they shoot?"

"I can't tell you that they won't. I don't think they will. But this is the only way through."

"Okay."

She is trembling. She is hungry, dehydrated and cold.

Sophie's newly cropped hair is wavy and dark and wildly frames her dirt-smeared face. Emil is again reminded of Talia. "Don't panic. Whatever you do. Trust me."

"I do."

Emil moves around the edge of the stone pile. Sophie walks closely beside him. The village is a collection of ravaged, rectangular, clay and wooden buildings. Fires burn near each structure. A group of people, the source of the chatter, is gathered near one of the fires. As she gets closer, Sophie sees that the people are covered in brightly coloured, woven garments. The men and the women wear baggy pants that taper at the ankles and short-waisted, thick vibrant coats of purple red and blue. On their heads they wear heavy woollen hats. Braided tassels hang from the hats over the ears of their wearers. The gathered have spotted the approaching strangers. Their conversation has stopped and they simply look on curiously.

Emil waves to put them at ease. He smiles and hopes for the best. Despite the circumstances, Sophie is intrigued by these gaily clad people living at the edge of modern society. She is absolutely enraptured with the appearance of them.

One of the men approaches. He removes his red, tasselled toque. His skin is rough and sunburnt, weathered from constant exposure to the elements. Emil extends a hand. The man reaches out to Emil and takes his hand, shaking it enthusiastically. This man seems to recognize Emil.

Emil speaks to this man in a language that Sophie does not understand. The man responds in a favourable tone, speaking excitably, it seems to Sophie. Then he turns and walks away.

"Does he know who you are?"

"Yes. He goes into Buena Gente to sell at the market. He knows my face."

"Is that good, Emil?"

"It seems so. He has invited us to eat."

Sophie feels a sense of hesitant buoyancy. She has eaten so little in the past day and a half, just berries and unripened fruits from the forest, and water from meagre streams whenever possible, teeming, no doubt, with every parasite imaginable. Not nearly enough to sustain life in the long term. The promise of a meal with these people is something to be happy about.

Sophie and Emil are shown past the group. Children scatter about them, but they are cautious and curious, not joyful. The remnants of damaged homes and the temporary chaos imposed by whatever attack these people faced are all about. The charcoal bleakness of the earth beneath their feet is a reminder that this is now a war zone.

They are welcomed into one of the small, rectangular buildings. The intoxicating smells of cooking delicacies waft from the entranceway—a small door frame with a thick blanket that serves as a door, pulled to one side and wrapped over a hook. Sophie and Emil are asked to sit on the floor with the children already seated. They are introduced, and Emil translates for Sophie. She listens to the foreign, rich and rolling syllables as Emil's voice transforms her words into the words of these people.

The home is warm, the ground is covered in hides of some sort, and they are soft and comfortable. Bowls are offered and accepted graciously. Sophie revels in the warm, hearty blandness of the meat stew. She doesn't care what it is that she is eating. Her belly accepts this nourishment indiscriminately. Emil speaks to the woman of the house. He translates his questions and the responses. He is asking her about the attacks on this village.

The man of the house excuses himself as Sophie and Emil are eating. The woman speaks of the surprise strike against the village. She refers to airplanes and loud explosions that were like fireworks set off from the ground. She says the explosions were caused by rockets that came from the planes. She believes it is because many from this village went away to fight with the militia in the wilderness. They want to free Perda from the foreign oppressors. They have guns, and rockets too. They want to be rewarded by their country for their bravery— just as does any soldier, fighting for a cause he or she believes in.

The woman's voice is hypnotic, though Sophie cannot understand her words.

The man is gone for some time.

When he finally returns, he is not alone.

§

The man returns with a soldier. A very tall man. He has to stoop to enter the small house. He has his weapon raised, but otherwise he does not speak or behave aggressively. He nods properly to the woman of the house as Emil and Sophie look on, realizing they have been exposed.

"Shit, shit, shit," Sophie curses quietly.

Emil carefully takes in the look of the soldier's uniform. This soldier is with the Alianza Central de Perda, an ally. "He's ACP. Just stay calm." Emil isn't sure what to make of this.

"Outside, please." The soldier steps aside for Sophie and Emil.

They stand. Sophie is reluctant, but Emil, his hand on her back, pushes her forward. "Just go," he whispers.

Sophie hesitantly walks past the soldier with Emil behind her. The soldier follows them out. The people of this village have gathered outside, but the soldier leads Sophie and Emil away from the crowd. He takes them to the other side of a waiting truck. It is large and covered in khaki fabric. Other soldiers wait inside the cab of this truck while the engine continues to whir.

The first soldier addresses Emil. "Emil Devante?"

Emil nods.

"Who is this?"

"I'm Sophie Panos. I'm a journalist."

"Papers?"

"No. I had them, but they are at my hotel. It was one of the hotels bombed this morning."

The soldier considers this while his gaze roams over Sophie. "What are you doing out here?"

Emil interjects. "We want to cross."

"You won't be allowed to leave the country. The border is guarded at every crossing now. Some of the stations are militia. You can't cross. Everyone in this country knows who you are. What are you doing out here?"

"I'd like to speak to your commander. I have critical information. In a camp, people are being held prisoner. The Adalardos. Bellona and Talia Adalardo." Emil has assumed a more authoritative stance, but the emotional surge in his voice when he speaks Talia's name belies his confidence. The campaign for reform was supported by the ACP, and although the means of the ACP were not publicly supported by the reformists, Emil's connection to Talia should have him in good standing with the ACP. Emil has clout, perhaps more than some. This soldier is too young to know this. Emil needs to speak with an officer.

The soldier ignores Emil's pleas. "You'll have to come with us. Get in." The soldier motions to the back of the truck.

"Not until I speak to a commanding officer."

"You will speak with an officer in Los Vientos." This is obviously the last bit of information the soldier will offer, at least for the time being.

"They are taking us to the ACP headquarters?" Sophie is hopeful.

Emil doesn't reply. Instead he watches the soldier for some sign of disquiet, insecurity. But this soldier is young, a drone, simply carrying out orders. Emil tries one last time to appeal to the boy's humanity. "Please, man. My family is in danger. I need to speak to someone now. I can't wait until we get to Los Vientos."

The soldier looks to one side for a moment before reconnecting his stare with Emil's. "You can use the satellite phone. It's not secure. You'll have to be brief."

The soldier goes to the cab of the truck and returns with the phone. He speaks into the receiver first, and then he hands it to Emil. "Go ahead, Mr. Devante."

§

Talia's vision is blurred. She is lying on her back, and looking at metal ceiling beams and the undersides of floorboards, as rust-coloured water oozes from pipes suspended by steel cables connected to the beams. She had believed that she would never open her eyes again. She had believed that the last thing she would see was the muzzle of the officer's pistol. But her eyes are open, and it doesn't make sense. Talia feels a sense of dread as she places her palms against her face. Her fingers press against her forehead, and then over the top of her head, the sides, and finally the back. She expects to find a wound, a gaping hole, blood, some indication of having been shot. She fears that she was shot after all, but obviously not fatally. She's heard stories of this happening—people being unaware of having just been wounded by a bullet. But she is not wounded. She has not been shot.

The action was a bluff on the officer's part, cruel entertainment. Talia had fainted upon hearing the landing of the gun's hammer. This is what she presumes. And now she has been returned to her cell. She is alone once again. She is alone. Her mother is dead. Her father is dead. Emil is probably dead or dying out there in the cold, and no one will help him because they are all too afraid for their own lives.

It seems impossible that life ever succeeds. That we begin as helpless creatures, entirely dependent on our fathers, our mothers. That we remain helpless for years and that we ultimately make it to adulthood. That a human body can sustain violence, emotional catastrophe, and the devastating loss of everyone who is important to it—this is astounding. Talia wants it all to be over. She tries to convince her body that its fight is over. It can let go. It can die. She wants it to. She doesn't want to live like this any more. She doesn't want the decision of her life or her death to be in the hands of her captors. She wants the decision to be hers. She'll choose when and how, not them. Talia's last rebellion will be this. She won't be used. She won't be tortured any longer. She won't let them do anything else to her, nor can she watch while they destroy others who are desperately holding on in this hell on earth. She wants to die on her own terms.

§

They are met by the commanding officer that Emil was speaking to en route. Upon seeing the state they are in, the stout, hardened, uniformed ACP commander immediately orders that they first be escorted to the infirmary. Emil protests. He asks question after question about the camp, about Talia, but the officer doesn't have any answers ... yet. He assures Emil that a visit to the infirmary will in no way slow the progress of the operation. The officer excuses himself temporarily. Emil and Sophie agree to be checked over. Emil enters the examination room first, while Sophie waits in a chair in the hallway outside.

Los Vientos is an isolated, industrial city that is only a city because it is called a city. Nothing else about this place is urban. It is a network of factories, refineries, storage facilities, pumps, housing facilities, trailers, restricted government and military sites. Dust storms whip up frequently in this arid, windy region and Sophie can feel the grit in the back of her throat, and in her teeth. She is so tired. Her body aches, she is dizzy from dehydration. She is relieved for her own safety, but she has come to care for Emil, to regard him as a friend. She has bonded with him in a way that only those who experience some crisis together might understand. He is in the darkest turmoil of his life because of the uncertainty surrounding Talia's life.

Sophie stares across the concrete floor of the ACP compound. The Alianza Central de Perda established itself when Perda first gained independence in the early twentieth century. In the beginning the alliance was formed in order to protect the newborn republic from future attempts at colonization. It was an alliance of heroes, of prominent military and governmental figures. Only in the past few decades has the ACP begun to stand for something completely different. The ACP alienated itself from the government—this alienation was especially indoctrinated during Bellona Adalardo's period of influence. Her government was elected almost unanimously in a historic election. And then attention on Perda's natural resources from abroad brought foreign interest, businesses, greed and scandal to Perda. The ACP now stands for reform, for violent opposition to the presence of foreign military in the region, and for extreme resistance to the Adalardo government's plans to allow a long-term military occupation, allegedly to secure Perda's economic future.

Sophie remembers the final briefing she received, the day before leaving for Perda. She was told that the Alianza Central de Perda was a disorganized, sectarian group and that they were the enemy of the occupation. The ACP is ferociously opposed to the occupation, but they are not the bloodthirsty zealots Sophie was told about, and they are not disorganized. The ACP is slowly restoring security to instable regions marred by truly sectarian militia violence, as well as anticipating—despite past criticism that their conjecture was paranoid—and fighting the invasion. The Alianza makes public its suspicions, many of which have been adopted by the purveyors of the campaign for reform. This was never a simple occupation intended to result in shared wealth. This was always going to be an invasion, according to the ACP, a takeover, hostile and fuelled by voracious ambition. And that is what has happened. Sophie sees the situation in Perda with newfound clarity and understanding, and with a sense of connectedness—synchronicity—that she embraces. She wants to be here, with these people. She wants to be in Perda, to fight alongside those opposed to the invasion. She needs to be among those who are committed to stopping the progress of naked aggression.

Emil emerges from the room. He seems unsettled.

"Is everything okay?" Sophie asks as she stands.

"I'm fine. The wound on my shoulder is infected. They've given me a shot for it. I'm just so … Sophie." Emil pauses. "She could be dead. I can't bear it if she's dead."

Sophie carefully hugs Emil. He rests his head on her shoulder. "Emil, Talia is smart, and strong. Everything you have told me about her, everything I already knew ... She'll find a way to survive. You need to believe that she will."

Emil pulls away. "She doesn't know that I got out. She was so upset about her mother."

"She won't give up, Emil. She won't give up if she thinks there is any chance that you are still alive. Trust in that."

He nods. "Has anyone been out to talk to you?"

"Not yet. I'm feeling okay. I'm sure it won't take them long to check me out." Sophie places her hand on Emil's forearm. Then she removes it and walks past him into the examination room.

The doctor is a young soldier. He is in uniform, no white coat. The room is a makeshift examination room cordoned off by dark green curtains that hang to the floor from metal racks. On the other side of the curtains Sophie can hear the buzz of

THE BEAUTY OF THE WORLD

whispered, heated discussions. There is a stool, a cabinet with glass doors in which medical supplies—gauze, bandages, syringes, small vials, glass bottles, alcohol, presumably sterile stainless steel instruments—are stored.

"Hello." The doctor addresses Sophie while patting the stool. "Please sit."

"Okay." Sophie moves over to the stool.

"You are a journalist?" The doctor touches her face, moving her head from side to side as he examines the scratches across her cheeks.

"Yes." Sophie is suddenly aware of how dirty she is. She explains this to the doctor.

He steps back and smiles. "Don't worry, I'm used to that."

"I had a headache. I hit my head, almost two days ago, after an explosion. It was the back of my head, against the door of a stationary truck."

"Anything other than a headache? Do you still have the headache?"

"I was sick to my stomach. I had a nosebleed, but the air was very dry. I had inhaled some smoke."

"Let's have a look." The doctor reaches behind Sophie's head and gently presses against her scalp, asking each time if she is feeling pain. She tells him that she doesn't.

He takes a penlight from his pocket and asks her to look straight ahead. She does. He shines the light intermittently over each eye. Sophie resists the urge to blink.

"Okay. Looks good. Let's just check the basics. Reflexes, pulse, blood pressure."

"Did I have a concussion?"

"A mild one probably, but you're all right now, it seems. No other symptoms?"

"I was dizzy when it first happened. And right now I'm really thirsty."

"We'll get you some water. Not dizzy any more?"

She shakes her head.

He wraps the rubber cuff of the sphygmomanometer around her arm and takes her blood pressure. Then he checks her heart rate and takes her pulse with his fingers on her wrist. "You're okay. Definitely dehydrated, though. Get some liquids in, not too much at a time. I'm just going to clean up some of these scratches you've got on your face."

"Do you know anything about the internment camps?" Sophie looks directly into the doctor's eyes as he applies cotton batten soaked in peroxide to one of the larger abrasions on her face.

"I've heard of them, of course. But I don't know anything about them really." He continues his work.

"How long have you been a part of the Alianza?"

"Not long, but long enough." He stands back. "Okay, you can go. Remember to drink."

Sophie nods and thanks him. She exits the room.

Emil is no longer in the hallway. Sophie starts toward the only other obvious room at the end of the hallway. The building is more of a bunker than a building.

"Sophie."

She turns back toward Emil. "I was looking for you."

"They've planned a rescue operation. They're going to the camp."

"Emil, that's good. When?"

"Today. Sophie, they're going to send you home. They'll get you out of the country first—"

"No. Emil, ... wait."

"Sophie, you aren't safe here. They can get you out. I'm going with them to the camp. They'll get you out of Perda this afternoon."

"No. That isn't what I want. I don't want to leave. I want to come to the camp."

Emil sees that Sophie is prepared to argue. He's confused. She is free, she can notify her colleagues, her family. But she hasn't mentioned the name of anyone to whom she is connected. "I don't understand. Don't you want to go home?"

"No. I don't know ... I don't want to leave Perda. I want to help."

"Why?"

"I don't have a reason. At least, not a reason I can explain. I want to help, that's all. It's important to me. I want to do something good here."

"I have to go."

"I want to come too. I want to come to the camp."

"Sophie, God. What are you talking about? You can't, they won't let you. It's too dangerous. The commander doesn't even want me there, but I know the layout of the camp. I have to go. I have to be there."

"Emil, they'll let me. I'm a reporter. Someone has to document this. Someone needs to get this stuff out into the world. Just tell me who to talk to."

She is so much like Talia, Emil thinks. She is careless, passionate, incorrigible and strong. He knows that he can't talk

Sophie out of this any more than he could talk Talia out of it if she was in front of him. "Commander Aitana."

"Let's go and speak to him."

Sophie follows Emil as he walks through the corridor and around a bend. They stop at the guarded doors where the commander is speaking to the guards. He turns to address them immediately.

"Good. We're ready to speak, then? Everyone is healthy, hmm?" The commander, now smiling, is more animated. "Please, inside." He gestures forward with his hand.

One of the guards enters a code into a keypad to the side of the doorway. Steel bars positioned horizontally across the entryway disengage and then the doors must be opened manually. Emil and Sophie are taken into a situation room. Maps are strewn across the table, as are aerial photos, black and white, presumably of various regions in Perda. In the centre of the table is a tray. On the tray is a pitcher of water with glasses. There is another tray beside it filled with fruit, bread and meats.

"Please, sit down. Eat while we talk."

Emil sits.

Sophie reaches forward for a glass of water, pours one for herself, and then pours another and places it in front of Emil. She too takes a seat. "Emil, drink."

He is moved by the simple command and he realizes that Sophie is looking out for him. He smiles and takes the glass of water.

The debriefing will be an hour or so and Emil and Sophie are to explain everything they know about the situation at the camp, which they will soon learn is actually one of three camps. Later it will be referred to as Camp 1, the only camp overtaken by the militia and no longer under the control of the occupying forces.

Many things are revealed during this exchange of information and Sophie convinces the commander that she can be of some use during the rescue. Despite Emil's concerns for her safety, she will go along and document the operation. The operation will begin in less than three hours. This assault team has been put together to rescue Talia and Bellona Adalardo and the others still interned in Camp 1.

Emil will lead the way to the camp. He will direct the gunmen as the helicopters approach their targets. He knows the layout of the camp too well.

§

Sophie is seated in the gut of the huge, martial attack helicopter. It is one of two on this mission. She was given a flat, heavy, metal seat cover to protect her from any bullets fired from the ground. She is positioned in the centre of the machine with gunmen on either side of her. She is wearing a protective vest, a helmet and safety goggles that give everything in her vision a slightly convex appearance. She is armed with a digital video camera loaned to her by one of the technical people at the ACP headquarters. Sophie knows that she is doing the right thing, but as the helicopters approach the region where the camp is located, she is afraid. She wonders if she is going to die. If so, she wants a bullet to pierce her amour and kill her instantly, for she is frightened mostly of suffering and of knowing that she is dying.

The heavy, thudding whirl of the rotor blades hums overhead and sends shudders throughout the body of the helicopter. Emil is seated beside her. He wears a headset that is attached to his helmet. He is speaking into the mouthpiece. The camp is coming into view, and just as the two helicopters churn over a hilled area of dense desert brush and near the camp, the lead helicopter lets off a round of fire. This fire is meant to warn, not to harm. It is meant to provoke, to create chaos, to give the interned one last chance to escape their oppressors, who will inevitably become desperate and even more homicidal at the thought of being captured.

The camp is in plain sight. Its inhabitants are scattering, and the gunfire is returned from soldiers on the ground. The pilot manoeuvres the machine in order to make it a more difficult target. One of the soldiers has pushed Sophie's head forward and she is hugging her torso to her legs. "Stay down!"

Emil can only watch. He too has been pushed forward, but he leans sideways while pressed to his thighs and he peers at the camp from above. The size of it surprises him. It is larger than he realized. He sees the barracks at the north end of the camp, and he imagines Talia inside. He is so afraid of what he will find, and yet he is most afraid of finding no evidence of her at all. Emil speaks into his headset.

"That is the main barracks, up ahead." Bullets glance off the body of the helicopter.

The pilot pulls them around. "Hit them!" The gunmen begin to let off rounds that spray the ground. The bullets strike the two guards firing from the ground as well as a small crew as they are attempting to load a rocket-propelled grenade. The guards crumple to the ground. The attack helicopter releases a high-impact, air-to-land missile. The explosion creates enough confusion and smoke that the lead chopper is able to land while the second stands by as cover.

As the first chopper lands, soldiers stream out readily and begin a firefight on the ground. The ACP soldiers are wearing gas masks, for they immediately begin dispensing tear gas canisters across the grounds.

Witnessing this confusion, processing the images, it is difficult: smoke, black and grey, billowing from isolated detonation points, the remains of people, recently killed, dead, or dying and badly damaged, soldiers shuffling across the earth toward additional targets, the interned nowhere to be seen, hiding in their inadequate shelters that might as well have transparent walls. And somewhere in all of this is Talia.

The advance is carried out efficiently, and in minutes the second chopper with Sophie and Emil aboard is ordered to land. Sophie and Emil are instructed to stay aboard until the pilot gives an all-clear, but before the chopper even touches down, soldiers perched on its haunches drop themselves to the earth and immediately scatter. They will search the tents and buildings for remaining hostiles.

Despite being instructed to wait, Emil descends to the earth with the soldiers. Sophie yells after him, but she knows she can't stop him. Sophie is already leaning forward. She is snapping digital photographs of the chaos around her. Using the camera, she records brief videos, during which she explains what she is seeing. The pilot signals to her, and Sophie removes her harness. The blades of the helicopter are no longer rotating. She pulls the camera bag across her chest and shoulder, and pushes herself out of the chopper.

The smoke on the grounds has dissipated into the air, but there is still enough present to cause Sophie's eye to burn, despite her goggles, which she promptly trades for a gas mask. The soldiers from the second chopper are searching the grounds. They are gathering the interned from their tents into the centre of the camp. The scene is like one from the Second World War. These people have been starved, beaten. They are barely living, barely able to carry themselves toward salvation.

The ACP soldiers are met with tears, hugs, prayers. People fall to their knees—this is deliverance for those who are still deliverable. The interned are being assembled, they are asked to remain calm. Their eyes are weary, their faces sallow, their bodies gaunt, undernourished and overstressed. Sophie photographs them, she speaks to some, and she ends up embracing others. These people are desperate to be treated once again as all human beings should be treated.

Emil knows that there is only one place Talia is likely to be. The barracks. The divisional fences have been cut open to allow the passage of the camp's liberators.

The barracks are in the third partition. Emil is running now. The one-storey building resembles an aircraft hangar from the exterior. The layout of it interior is an unknown. This building holds secrets, its inhabitants the elusive, brutal figures that remained nameless, compassionless and conscienceless throughout the ordeal of the camp.

Emil approaches the building. He is breathing heavily. When he is close enough, he pauses. The ACP soldiers are gathered on the wooden stairs into the building.

"Have you been inside?" he asks one of the soldiers.

The soldier turns to Emil as though he understands the depth of Emil's question. "You can go inside yourself. It's secure. Wear this." The soldier removes his own brightly coloured vest and passes it to Emil. "Just in case. Some of our guys are inside. You don't want them thinking you're one of the bad guys."

Emil thanks him. Pulls the vest on and ascends the stairs. He isn't prepared to find Talia. He isn't prepared *not* to find her.

When he gets to the doors, he opens them and finds himself inside a short hallway. It opens onto the main corridor of the barracks. He steps forward, one foot after the other, one breath after another; he is perhaps just one moment away from absolute relief or absolute devastation. There is a part of him that doesn't want to know any more. A part of him that wants to hope, forever.

The barracks are darkened; daylight streams in through slats in the walls. The doors are open to eliminate the tear gas that was used. The visor to Emil's mask is fogging up. He is perspiring and breathing rapidly. He moves forward with his hands in plain sight. He doesn't know where to begin, and so he begins at one end and moves slowly toward the other. He moves past the ghostly forms of ACP soldiers. He stops and asks about survivors, anyone who is not one of the hostiles. The soldiers shake their heads and continue with their task of pushing the bodies of hostiles into piles against one of the walls. Emil pauses each time he sees a body. He looks over each lifeless being, but none is Talia.

Bunk-style, stacked beds line the wall, and in recessed portions of the walls are doorways that lead to tiny, makeshift offices. Emil opens the doors to these rooms and finds nothing in them but overturned furniture and discarded items. He marvels that these people were able to terrorize the interned from this ragged, disorganized hub.

He is nearing the end of the long corridor. He opens the door to a large room. He enters and finds shelves of supplies, foodstuffs, industrial-sized sinks and a large wood oven and stove. A section of this room belongs to long tables where these soldiers would have taken their meals—a reminder that even the darkest among us must eat, sleep, eliminate waste, and perform the other quotidian tasks associated with the physical needs of being human.

There are bodies in this room, but none is female.

Emil finds a door that leads to a stairwell. He takes the stairs down into a room that smells of earth and must—a cold-storage room. He knows this because he feels the familiar shapes of fruits, vegetables, open bags of rice. The cool, damp air is filled with the scent of rotting produce. Emil hears the scurrying of creatures underfoot. He is careful not to extend his hands too near to the floor or into any dark crevices, although he doubts that snakes would inhabit a space as cold as this. There is a door frame built into one of the walls of this room. But Emil does not find it. This door leads to the larger part of the underground of this building, the lower cells of the barracks.

Emil returns to the main corridor. He finds his way into one of the last small rooms. In this room, a dead man is fallen backward in his chair behind a desk. The man wears a blue uniform, the same uniform as the Perdan Special Forces. In his rigidly clenched right hand he grips a pistol. Emil is glad that this man took his own life, Emil hopes it was painful, he hopes that this man suffered for a time before dying of his self-inflicted wound.

Emil goes back into the hallway. At the end of the corridor is a doorway. Emil walks toward the last possible place in this building where Talia might be found. He tries to open the door. It won't budge. It is a large metal door, with great hinges that are difficult to undo. He pulls at them until his fingers are bleeding, and finally they give. The door opens up to reveal a narrow, naturally lit passage, more slatted windows. In the dim light, Emil finds another staircase. He knows from the smell what he is about to find.

He descends into the underground again and before he reaches the bottom of the steps he sees five bodies, obviously dead for some time, for the stench is unbearable. He vomits uncontrollably in a corner of the room. Two of the bodies are of women, lying face down, their arms and legs bent unnaturally but the shapes of their hips and waists a clear indication of their sex. Emil's hand is over his mouth, but the new vomit rising in his throat has nothing to do with the stench. He is pinned against the wall by grief. He prays to anyone who will listen, to be sure that all the gods and demons are satisfied so as not to leave any lurking. He prays that by some miracle, neither of these women will be Talia.

§

Bellona watches as Talia leaves the lavatory. She knows she has just laid eyes on her daughter for the last time. The room is empty. The other women—able to stand by while she was raped but unable, or unwilling to help her after the assault—have left. Bellona cannot keep her promise to Talia. She will not hide in another tent and wait, for Bellona is not going to live anyway, not without medical intervention. She feels the blood leaving her body and she knows she must act before she no longer has the strength.

She pulls herself up and, leaning against the tiled wall, pulls her body along. She stands on her own, for she has to. She has to walk from the lavatory to the barracks, a distance of about two hundred metres.

Bellona closes her eyes. She begs for help, for strength, just enough to do what she has to. Bellona can't undo what she has already done. She has failed, as a wife, as a mother. She has failed her country. She has failed in her life in every way that matters to her. She won't fail in this last task.

She moves forward and exits the lavatory. With the smallest of steps, she slowly moves toward her destination. Each step leaves her less stable, weaker and more frightened for Talia. Bellona is all but crawling when she manages to find her way to the wooden stairs leading up to the barracks.

The guard looks at her. He shakes his head and reluctantly helps her up. "What do you want? Go back to your tent." He begins to turn her around.

"Please, wait. I have information."

He stops and pushes her away to look at her. "Information about what?"

"I am Bellona Adalardo."

She can tell from the expression on his face that he might recognize her.

"Go back to your tent."

"No, please. Take me inside. They will tell you who I am when they see me. They will want to speak to me."

He considers this. "Wait here."

She waits. The guard goes inside and returns with an officer who, upon seeing her and knowing what he knows, verifies her identity. "Bring her inside."

"I can't walk," she says.

The guard grudgingly lifts her and brings her inside. He carries her the length of a corridor and into a room where another officer sits. The guard roughly pushes her into a chair. Bellona nearly loses consciousness, but she holds on.

The officer behind the desk stands. "Do you remember me?"

Bellona looks at him with blurred vision. "I don't have a lot of time to tell you what you want to know."

He steps around the desk and surveys her injuries. "What's wrong with you?"

"I'm bleeding, badly."

"Why?"

"Ask your guards."

He smiles. "So what do you want, then?"

"You know my daughter is here." She doesn't wait for him to reply. "I'll give you information, classified information, if you promise to keep Talia alive." Bellona leans forward, her brow beaded with sweat and her breathing shallow. The room is closing in around her.

He considers her proposition. "And what makes you think that I won't kill her after she gives us this information?"

Bellona speaks with her head down and her eyes closed. "I don't think that you are monsters. You believe in what you are doing, and I have no choice but to trust you." Bellona looks up at him. "Besides, she is worth so much more to you alive."

The officer sees that Bellona is hardly the same woman she was just months before. She is no longer powerful, no longer strong, and she is the reason behind this country's collapse. If only the people of Perda could see their fallen leader now, bargaining with governmental secrets for the life of her only child.

Bellona will tell this man whatever he wants to hear, as long as it buys her enough time to keep Talia alive for just a few days. Just long enough for Emil and Pierre to find her, somehow. Bellona knows of the love that Emil has for Talia. She knows that he will find a way to her. She looks at the officer who has not yet spoken.

"Please. I give you my life for hers."

§

Sophie makes her way slowly through the camp. She has lifted her mask up over her head, where it rests purposelessly, in the way. She steps carefully around the debris scattered across the grounds. Her heart is breaking for these people. Their minds, their souls, their bodies, their ideas: they have been ravaged, violated, compromised beyond the limits of human endurance, and yet they are here, alive.

Sophie steps through a gate in one of the fences that divides the sections of this camp. All around her the survivors are gathered, but she doesn't stop to speak with any others, for she's heard too much. Reading about atrocities in texts is far different from first-hand accounts of recent, unimaginable suffering. She wants to help every one of these people, she wants to hold every one of them, and she wants to undo everything that has happened to them. But then she chastises herself for this, because these wants are about *her* feelings. She can't stand the idea that this was allowed to happen. The sadness she is feeling is as much about her own place in the world as it is about acknowledging the anguish that these people have experienced. She walks toward one of the buildings in this section, walks through an open door. It is a lavatory. The abrupt rankness of the air in the large, tiled room, the sight of the conditions, it is too much. Sophie cannot go any farther. She turns back toward the cleaner, outside air, and she is grateful for the congestion in her nose and throat caused by the tear gas. She takes a deep gulp, and then turns in to the room once again. She begins shooting images of the soiled, disgusting floor, the walls smeared with the history of brutality carried out in this place, the remnants of clothing discarded in a corner.

She exits the lavatory, takes a moment before selecting the video option on the camera. She turns the camera on herself and addresses the lens and tells the story of what she has seen thus far.

When she is finished, she crouches for a moment, her elbows resting on her knees, and she glances around her. She looks toward what seems to be the largest building on the grounds. There on its steps sits Emil with his head in his hands. Sophie fears the worst as she pulls herself together and begins her pilgrimage to where he is seated. And then she is beside him, resting her hand on his shoulder.

Emil looks up at her. "I found Bellona, and another woman, underground, in a bunker. But not Talia."

Sophie nods. "They're ..."

"Yes."

"My God. I'm sorry, Emil. How awful."

"She should have been here."

Sophie sees that he is giving up. "Emil, go and look for her. You don't know that they took her in here for sure. Go and speak to the others."

"I don't want to know any more. I don't want to hear them say it. I don't ever want to know, Sophie." He begins to weep, releasing everything that he is feeling. His tears are profuse and unrelenting. "I don't want to know." His head is once again in his hands.

Sophie stands; she squeezes his shoulder, in a way that tells him that she cares and that she will be back in a moment.

She starts up the steps, she enters the barracks, and she begins to photograph all of it. The corridor, the stacks of beds along the walls, the empty offices that contain everyday machines and materials found in any other office anywhere in the world. In some spaces she finds the bodies of hostiles and she photographs them too. She wonders if there is a hell after all, if so, it has inspired the monsters in this camp.

The smoke is barely perceptible now, but Sophie's eyes are stinging. It is much easier for her to use the camera and to speak into it when she shoots video footage, without the gas mask on.

Sophie finds one of the ACP soldiers in an office where a man behind a desk has shot himself in the head. Sophie takes a picture, of the man's face, his hand still holding the pistol, his empty gaze and the uniform he is wearing. Then she takes a shot of the ACP soldier, and she asks him some questions. She wants to interview him. He agrees, and Sophie shoots a short video including his comments on the grisly scene in the room.

Sophie asks the ACP soldier if he might accompany her as she walks the corridor from end to end. She asks if he will hold the camera for her as she documents the situation. He agrees. They begin at this end of the corridor, and slowly she walks the as-yet-to-be-determined audience through the barracks as she carefully describes everything she is seeing. She investigates and photographs every crevice, every room and even the pictures hung on the walls beside some of the beds.

Finally they are at the other end of the corridor. Sophie thanks the soldier for his help. He asks her if he will be on television, and she tells him that she hopes the whole world will see this. He seems pleased.

The camera's batteries are running low. Sophie drops the camera bag on the floor and bends to root through the bag for additional batteries. As she searches, she sees the contour of what appears to be a door in the floor. She pushes her bag aside, and brushes the dust from the floor. There is a recessed handle that she lifts and turns, but the door is too heavy for her to lift open. She struggles with it before calling the soldier back over to help her. Together they pry the door open and the soldier orders Sophie to stand aside. He readies his weapon, he speaks into his radio, and then he instructs her to wait. Sophie complies, for a moment, but then, leaving her bag and camera behind, she follows him down the steep concrete steps into a dark passageway. The soldier snaps on a flashlight and Sophie lets him know that she is behind him. He whispers harshly for her to go back and wait. But she refuses. Sophie continues behind him. They are in a corridor, to the side of which are fenced in cages, *cells*.

The soldier flashes his light into each as they pass by, but the cells are empty. They have passed seven or eight cells when the soldier curses under his breath. Sophie looks to the side, toward where the soldier has his flashlight pointing. There in the dimness of the torchlight is the body of a woman. She is on her side, her legs curled into her chest, her arms wrapped protectively around her head.

Sophie knows that this is Talia. She *feels* that this is Talia. "No," she says aloud without realizing that she has spoken.

"Hold this." The soldier pushes the flashlight into Sophie's hand, lowers his weapon and moves to open the cell door. It gives way without force. He bends down and places his hand against the woman's face and neck. At first he is moving with sympathetic slowness, but then he presses his fingers into her neck with more purpose and urgency. Sophie doesn't believe it when he turns to tell Sophie that the woman is alive.

Sophie enters the cell and kneels next to the woman's body. She carefully moves the woman onto her back as the soldier speaks into his radio. Sophie is shaken by the woman's fragile condition. The woman's arms and legs are so thin that boney corners are apparent beneath her tattered clothing. The woman is cradling the sides of her head, cradling her memories perhaps, protecting herself from this dark reality. Sophie smooths the woman's hair from her face, which is bruised, bloody and obviously beaten. She bends to the woman's ear.

"Talia?"

The woman does not move.

Sophie tries repeatedly, whispering *Talia* over and over, her hand still resting against the woman's face.

Sophie has turned away for a moment while other soldiers make their way into the passageway. Sophie hears their voices as they approach.

"Please ..." says the woman.

Sophie turns back. The woman's eyelids are moving. Her mouth is forming words that do not seem to be able to find her voice.

THE BEAUTY OF THE WORLD

Sophie begins to cry when she hears the woman's voice offered to her. "Talia?"

"Yes. Yes. Yes." The woman is crying softly. "Please."

"Talia, my name is Sophie. I'm here to help. It's okay now. Everything's okay." Sophie softly moves Talia's hands away from her head. Sophie holds them in hers to warm them.

Talia cannot open one of her eyes, but the other eyelid she peels back reluctantly, squinting in the brightness of the flashlight. The noise of voices is all around her. She focuses on the sound of this woman's voice beside her.

"Talia, listen to me. You are safe. Emil is safe. He's here with us, he is here for you."

Talia hears these words. She hears these words. *She hears these words.* Emil. Emil is here. Emil is alive. I am alive. Emil. These are Talia's thoughts as they carefully lift her. She holds herself against the chest of a strange man, his arms under her knees and around her body. She welcomes the light as she is carried into the main corridor and lowered gently onto one of the closest bunks.

Sophie follows this procession up the steps to where Talia is laid. Talia's eyes are once again closed, but she repeats Emil's name in hoarse, tortured murmurs. The soldier that has carried her is now pulling a blanket over her. Another soldier has arrived and is taking her pulse, looking into her eyes, asking her questions.

"Emil." Talia's voice is now louder, purposeful, and she looks at Sophie.

THE BEAUTY OF THE WORLD

Sophie nods, reaches down and places her hand comfortingly on Talia's blanketed arm. Then she turns and makes her way out to find Emil.

As she exits the barracks, she sees that Emil is no longer seated on the steps. Sophie knows that he is searching the tents for some sign of Talia. Searching. Hoping. Loving. Desperate. Afraid. And in moments she will tell Emil the news, and she is feeling almost buoyant while surrounded by the scene of the liberated camp. Sophie knows that there is formidable strength, passion and resolve in these people. In Talia, who has lived for Emil.

Sophie would like to speak to Talia about much, and someday she will. Perda has been so many things to Sophie. She will stay here. Until this war has ended, and after that too.

Sophie walks the grounds. The rescued are huddled together in the distance, for warmth perhaps, but mostly in a collective expression of absolute, exhausted gratitude, for they have survived something that so many did not. It will be many years before they heal fully from this ordeal, and some will never recover. Sophie considers the past days, Tom's death, her journey through the Perdan forest and mountains, her conversations with Emil. She considers her life, and everything that she thought she understood before coming here, before Perda. Those ideas seem foreign to her now.

As she rounds the lavatory building, she finally sees Emil some distance away. He is speaking to a soldier, his back turned.

As Sophie makes her way to him, he turns and faces her, still speaking He does not immediately make anything of her presence. He had expected that she would come looking for him after exploring the barracks. But then Emil stops mid-sentence. He has noticed the expression on her face.

Sophie feels herself smiling. Not just smiling, she is laughing and crying by the time she reaches him. She pulls Emil to her and wraps her arms around him and holds him as tightly as she can and knows he can't believe the words as she whispers them into his ear.

Talia.

Epilogue

PERDAN WAR STATISTICS

Duration of conflict (approximate)	39 months
Reconstruction time (approximate)	8 years
Total Service Members (worldwide)	963,000
Battle Deaths (theatre)	22,450
Non-Combatant Deaths (approximate)	57,340
Other Deaths in Service (non-Theatre)	237
Non-mortal Woundings	104,234
Number of Peacekeeping Forces Deployed to Perda	34,000
Internment Camp Casualties:	Total: 1,294

CAMP 1 *: 1,269 including 196 children (remains discovered in mass grave, causes of deaths unspecified)
CAMP 2: 14 (natural causes)

CAMP 3: 11 (natural causes)

Other Facts

The largest number of war criminals prosecuted and convicted by the Global War Crimes Court ever documented: Charges brought about due to the invasion of Perda based on fabricated evidence and false pretences.

The invasion of Perda established a precedent whereby unsanctioned invasions of territories that are carried out against the recommendations of the United Nations will be considered as acts of war against all members of the United Nations. Each member nation supplies volunteer military personnel according to a percentage per capita for each nation. These military reserves receive refresher training annually and are ready for deployment in any area of the world when necessary. These military personnel do not include the increased force of UN Peacekeepers now deployed to troubled areas of the world. Peacekeepers are now given the power to intervene appropriately if non-combatant lives are endangered. This shift in UN policy is a direct result of the high number of civilian casualties during the invasion of Perda.

The war in Perda prompted an unprecedented movement by journalists refusing to work for certain networks on coverage of the invasion. Although the boycott was not successful due to a lack of participation, it prompted the formation of the International Media Committee, composed of representatives from any nation that wishes to participate. This group does not carry any governing power; however, it does exist to expose media coverage that is inflammatory, blatantly false and/or considered to be designed to incite hate crimes. Many networks around the world have embraced the IMC's recommendations; however, many international networks are strongly opposed to the group. This is an ongoing world issue.

* Camp 1 was originally established with Camps 2 and 3. These internment camps were planned and established jointly by the Adalardo Government and the Coalition of Nations for the Occupation of Perda. However, approximately six weeks after the internment camps began operating; Camp 1 was overtaken by a group of militia formed by dissidents of the occupying forces and the Alianza Central de Perda (the ACP), as well as some civilian insurgents. It is suspected, and in some cases known, that the majority of the deaths that occurred in Camp 1 were a result of extermination practices.

Acknowledgments

The writing of a novel is a fanatical process, undertaken by the author, but supported by people in the author's life who provide the staples that sustain creativity: constant encouragement, advice, space when needed, criticism, interest, understanding, and love. There are so many people to thank for their contributions to the writing of *The Beauty of the World*.

Thank you: To Allyson Latta for her comprehensive and supportive editing and for helping me to find my story. To Lara Chauvin, a gifted artist and friend, for reading this novel and painting such an exquisite depiction of Talia for the cover of the book.

To Stephen for the many hours of reading, rereading, keeping quiet, giving me space when I needed it and for his unfailing love. To CHM, with love. To Jen for always encouraging me to follow my dreams, for listening, and for epitomizing friendship. And to my mother.

Finally, to all my generous colleagues, friends, family and supporters who are too numerous to mention by name; I hope that I have demonstrated my appreciation for your efforts with as much enthusiasm as you have shown regarding my work.

About the Author

STACEY NEWMAN attended Sheridan College and the University of Toronto where she studied History and English. Stacey has been writing since she was a little girl. She began her freelancing career at twenty. This is her first published novel. Her past publishing credits include short stories & poems, as well as regular contributions to a number of Canadian magazines. She lives near Toronto, ON with her husband.

About the Cover

"Talia" was painted by Lara Chauvin in 2004 after reading *The Beauty of the World.*

BY THE ARTIST:
I was born in Sydney, Australia to Armenian parents, and grew up in diametrically opposed cultures; from the laid back Aussie mindset to the proud, traditional beliefs of the Armenian culture. Fascinated with illustration, design and painting from an early age, instead of pursuing art as a full time career or level of study, I ended up studying Fashion Illustration & Design. After 8 years in the 'Rag Trade' working with design identities, corporate retail giants, as well as backstage at some international events, I landed in the infamous Brett Whiteley Studio in Sydney where I finally felt I was at home. This is where I started a unique transition, re-inventing myself back to my original intention, at the same time meeting my husband & moving to Canada.

One of my recent bodies of work concentrates on deconstructing the perfection of beautiful women in today's society who often have such dark lives, secrets or untold stories. I often place them against a solid background with sgraffito text or in "Talia's" case a slight indication of a barrier such as the barbed wire, usually incorporating dark outlines & heavy shadows, in hopes to make the viewer concentrate on the expression, rather then being diverted & distracted by a detailed background.

Recently nominated for the Mayor's Evening Award for "Emergent Artist" in Edmonton Canada, I am ready with a fresh canvas to pursue my life long desire to become a serious artist, whilst extending & maintaining my hand in areas such as Children's & Book illustration.

www.larachauvin.com